Neil was still hand **wavy hair and ch** **the hint of a dimple on his firm jaw... But this was *her* big story. Period.**

"I hope I'm not interrupting your investigation," Kate said.

"No," Neil said. "We don't think Mr. Riley killed his wife, largely for two reasons. We didn't find any gunshot residue on him, and we haven't found the weapon."

Kate had known that sooner or later she'd have to face Neil again, but somehow she'd managed to avoid thinking about this moment. "If he did it, how did he get rid of the gun?"

"That's the question." Neil shook his head. "And if he did do it, we should have found residue on his hands and his clothes. We've been through all that. It had to be an outsider."

"Were the Christmas presents opened?" Kate said. With only a month under her belt at the *Portland Press Herald*, this might be just the break she needed to prove herself. "The Rileys' Christmas packages. The gun could be in one of them."

Books by Susan Page Davis

Love Inspired Suspense

Just Cause
Witness
On a Killer's Trail

SUSAN PAGE DAVIS

is a native of central Maine. She and her husband, Jim, have six children and five grandchildren. Susan has many years of experience as a freelancer for a daily newspaper. Her books include eight historical novels, two children's books and several romantic suspense. She writes cozy mysteries with her daughter, Megan. Visit Susan's Web site at www.susanpagedavis.com.

Susan Page Davis
ON A KILLER'S TRAIL

Steeple
Hill®

Published by Steeple Hill Books™

STEEPLE HILL BOOKS

Steeple
Hill®

Recycling programs
for this product may
not exist in your area.

ISBN-13: 978-0-373-44325-3
ISBN-10:   0-373-44325-0

ON A KILLER'S TRAIL

Copyright © 2009 by Susan Page Davis

Printed in U.S.A.

A righteous man regardeth the life of his beast:
but the tender mercies of the wicked are cruel.
—*Proverbs* 12:10

To Neil and Bex, an intrepid couple I'm proud
to be related to. May God bless you richly
in your life together.

Acknowledgment

My deepest thanks to Neil Roosma, who gave me
a crash course in things Dutch; to my husband Jim,
who patiently drove me around Portland as we
scouted the perfect scene of the crime; the kids in
the backseat, who didn't complain too much; and
Paige Winship Dooly, who kindly critiqued the
manuscript for me.

ONE

On Christmas morning, reporter Kate Richards studied the old Federal-style brick house as she approached it, letting her compact car roll slowly down the street behind police captain Connor Larson's forest-green Explorer. This was going to be a huge story. She could feel it.

Connor pulled into the sloping driveway and parked behind a black pickup truck and a marked squad car. A second police car was parked on the street, ahead of Kate. Connor, the head of a special detective unit for the Portland Police Department, got out of his SUV and walked back to where she'd pulled to the curb.

Kate lowered her window. Connor leaned down to talk to her.

"That's Neil's truck."

"Great." She bit her lip. Was she ready to meet Neil Alexander again?

"You okay?"

She pulled out a smile she didn't feel. "Sure."

Connor inhaled slowly. "I shouldn't have brought you, Kate. You know that."

"Oh, come on, Connor. I promise I'll do whatever you say."

"Really?"

"Really."

"Because I'm your brother-in-law?"

"No, because you're the officer in charge of this investigation. I told you I'd wait out here until you came and told me I could come closer. I brought my laptop, and I'll do some work while I wait." She was new on the job at the biggest newspaper in Maine, and this weekend she was on call for breaking stories, even though it was a holiday. She'd gone ahead with her Christmas plans to visit Connor and her sister, Adrienne, but she was never far from her cell phone and laptop, just in case. When the call came in telling of a possible homicide, she'd begged her brother-in-law to give her access to the scene.

Now, Connor looked her in the eye for a long moment, nodded and walked up the driveway through the new snow. He made an impressive figure in his dark overcoat. Tall, broad-shouldered, with short, crisp hair and glasses. He looked the way a captain of police detectives should. One of these days, she would ask him if she could write a profile on him for the Sunday paper. He'd probably say no.

Kate caught her breath as a tall, dark-haired young man came down the steps and met Connor in the yard. Neil. She recalled her impression when she first met him six months ago: he couldn't possibly be a detective. A man that handsome could never blend in with a crowd for undercover work.

He never looked her way as he and Connor talked together in the driveway for a couple of minutes. Connor bent down and seemed to be looking hard at the steps. He straightened, and the two of them entered the house together.

Kate exhaled, took out her phone and keyed in the newspaper's number. The copy editor stuck with holiday duty answered.

"Hey, Darrin. This is Kate Richards again. I'm at the scene of the crime. The officer in charge says that if I wait, I'll get my story, so I'm waiting."

"I dunno, Kate." Darrin sounded sleepy or bored. "You're a rookie."

"I can do this."

"Maybe I should call John."

"No, don't do that." Kate straightened her shoulders, her mind racing. "The city editor would really hate it if you called him on Christmas morning. You know that, right?"

"Well…we don't usually put newbies on a major crime story, especially a murder."

"Come on, Darrin. Nobody wants to come in to work today. I'm the reporter on call, and I got the tip. Don't pull this out from under me. Please."

"What's it worth to you?"

Kate gulped, cataloging her meager assets. A thought struck her that just might work. "Do you have New Year's Eve off?"

"I wish. You mean you'd take me to a party?"

"No. But I know something that might help you get the night off."

"Tell me."

"Promise you won't put another reporter on this?"

After a short pause, he said, "Whatever."

"Stephanie Leigh told me as she was going out the door yesterday that her husband can't get New Year's Eve off. She said, 'I might as well work, too.' If she hasn't traded with anyone else yet, you might be able to make a deal."

"That's not much."

"Call her and ask."

"Okay, I will."

Darrin hung up. Kate felt none-too-secure in her position covering the murder case, but it was the best she could do on short notice. If she started to rough out the story, maybe that would help sway the editor. She rummaged in her oversize purse and came out with a small notebook and a pen. Looking at the brick house, she jotted impressions of the architecture, the neighborhood, the mood. Her first big story, maybe. If Darrin didn't yank it out from under her. With only a month under her belt at the *Portland Press Herald,* this might be just the break she needed to prove herself. She banished all thoughts of Neil from her mind. Time to think about him later.

She stretched to reach her leather computer case from the backseat. It was a long shot that she'd find anything pertinent, but it was worth a try. She brought up a search engine and typed in the address of the old brick house. Bingo. She smiled and scrolled down, reading with avid interest.

"Too bad so many people have been in and out of the house." Connor frowned at the footprints on the snowy steps.

"Yeah," Neil said. "When I got here, three cops had already gone in. I couldn't make out anything from the prints." He nodded to the uniformed officer stationed at the door, then said a quick prayer for the victim's family as he and Connor entered the house. Stairs rose from the small entry, with balsam fir branches woven along the banister. To the right, an arch opened into a formal living room. Greenery hung all around the room, and a clump of mistletoe dangled from the chandelier. Boughs and red candles graced the mantel, amid china figurines and a large case clock. A heap of wrapped presents lay mounded beneath a decorated spruce that nearly scraped the high ceiling. The ornaments on that tree could have stocked a small gift shop.

All of the decorations and the antique furniture were eclipsed by the body lying facedown on the Oriental rug. Patrol officer Elaine Bard was examining the murder victim but she stood when Connor and Neil walked in. Another officer knelt on the other side of the body, and a third patrolman stood talking to a white-haired man seated on an Empire-style sofa near the windows that overlooked Westbrook Road.

"Captain Larson," Elaine said, nodding toward Connor and Neil. "Your case?"

"Yes," said Connor, pulling on latex gloves. "What do we have?"

"Sixty-eight-year-old woman, Edna Riley, found here by her husband, Mr. Gerald Riley." She nodded toward the sofa. "He thought she was ill, but when he tried to turn her over, he discovered a chest wound. I've called the medical examiner."

"They're the only two in the house?"

"Yes, but Mr. Riley says he expects their son and his family any minute. They were going to spend the weekend here. Coming up from Dover, New Hampshire, this morning."

Neil and Connor knelt and looked at Mrs. Riley. Her thinning gray hair was curled tightly around her forehead. She was a little plump, not too heavy, just a grandmotherly sort of woman. Neil glanced over at Mr. Riley, and saw his calm desert him as reality set in. Tears streamed down his cheeks, and the other officer, Pete Downey, handed him a handkerchief.

Neil took pictures to document the position of the body. Connor slipped on gloves and carefully rolled Mrs. Riley onto her left side so he could examine the wound.

"No exit wound. Small-caliber pistol," he hazarded.

"Got her in the heart?" Neil asked.

"Yeah."

"Powder burns on the front of her housecoat." Neil mulled that over. Someone had been standing within three feet of Mrs. Riley when he or she pulled the trigger. He asked Elaine Bard, "Any sign of the weapon?"

"I didn't find anything," she said. "I don't think it's under her."

Connor and Neil felt carefully along the length of the body and found nothing.

"Okay, Neil, Elaine and Joe, start looking for evidence. I'll speak to Mr. Riley." Connor took Mr. Riley and patrolman Pete Downey into another room.

As the ranking officer remaining, Neil took charge. "All right, we'll start right here. Bag and label anything you find." He, Elaine and Joe carefully examined every inch of the Oriental rug and the polished hardwood floor around the perimeter of the room. Joe shined his flashlight up the chimney.

After five minutes or so, the patrolman from outside came in. "Where's the captain?" he asked.

Neil gestured across the hall.

Connor came out of the room opposite. "What is it, Kevin?"

"The son's here, with his wife and four kids."

Connor sighed. "Ask young Mr. Riley to come in alone, please, and show him into the family room."

Kevin nodded. "Oh, and that woman in the red car is still out there."

"Don't worry about her. She's fine."

Neil said nothing, but he glanced at Connor curiously.

When the patrolman went out, Connor said, "Mr. Riley doesn't think either his prints or his wife's are in the system. Get the kit from my Explorer and take Mr. Riley's prints. Check for powder burns, too." He tossed Neil his keys and went back into the side room.

"Will you take her prints?" Elaine asked, nodding toward the corpse.

"They'll get them at the morgue," Neil said.

He left Elaine and Joe to finish searching the room. Outside, he unlocked Connor's vehicle and lifted out the fingerprint kit. The red car that had followed Connor to the scene was still parked at the curb, the engine running. A striking brunette sat in the driver's seat, watching him.

Kate Richards.

His heart lurched. What was she doing here?

Neil was tempted to go over and speak to her, but decided against it. Their last meeting hadn't been cordial. He was sure Connor would enlighten him as to the reason for Kate's presence if he asked. He nodded in her direction without making eye contact again and went inside.

Gerald Riley was meek and cooperative as Neil fingerprinted him and tested his hands for gunshot residue. The old man's son was talking to Connor, a stricken look on his face that mirrored his father's. When Neil went back to the living room, Elaine and Joe were gingerly moving every package out from under the Christmas tree and piling them up carefully to one side. Neil helped them examine the area under the tree and then put them all back. The arrangement didn't look as good as it had before, and Elaine fussed about it, moving a box here and there.

Connor came back in as they finished. "The son and his

family are going to a hotel. They'll take Mr. Riley with them for today and probably overnight. He didn't think they would want to sleep here, which will make things easier on us. What did you find?"

"Nothing, basically," Neil said. "No weapon in this room."

Kevin Dryer came to the door. "The M.E.'s here, sir."

"About time," said Connor.

Dr. McIntyre came in, muttering sourly, "Corpses on Christmas." He set his soft black bag down on the rug beside the body. "What happened here, Larson?"

Connor knelt on the other side of the body. "Looks like a small-caliber gunshot wound, sir."

"I don't suppose you found a gun?"

"No, sir."

"Nothing as easy as that, eh? What time?"

"Her husband found her just before nine o'clock—estimates five minutes to nine. He'd seen her fifteen minutes before, upstairs. She came down to start coffee for a late breakfast. When he came downstairs, she wasn't in the kitchen and didn't answer him, so he started looking around and found her like this."

"Did you move her?"

"Just lifted her a little to see where the wound was and if there was a weapon under her. That's the position she was in. My detective got photos."

McIntyre grunted and went on with his exam. After half a minute, Elaine started looking a little green and turned away. Connor took a call on his cell phone and walked over toward the windows.

"Excuse me." The son was in the archway.

Neil quickly moved to him. "I'm sorry, sir, it's better if you don't come in here."

"Of course." He looked down. "Is that the medical examiner?"

"Yes." Neil tried to stand where he would block the man's view.

"May I see my mother when he's finished?"

"It would be better if you wait. Let the funeral home take her. Do you and your father have a preference on where she should go?"

"I'll ask Dad."

"This is a preliminary exam," Neil explained. "The M.E. will probably take the body for a full autopsy. After that, he'll call the funeral home to come and get her."

"All right. I'll help my father pack a few things, and we'll go to the hotel," Riley said.

"I think that would be best," Neil told him.

Riley went back to the family room.

Connor ended his phone conversation and approached Neil.

"Did you ask young Mr. Riley about weapons?" Neil asked.

Connor nodded. "He says his father never owned a gun. Mr. Riley is a retired professor. Bookish man. Never hunted or anything."

"So you think someone came in from outside?"

"Could be. Gerald Riley says the front door was closed and locked when he discovered his wife's body, though. He had to flip the dead bolt to let the first officers in."

"So no one could have gone out the front door and locked it behind them without a key?"

"Right. You and Joe check all doors and windows. Unfortunately, a million people have gone in and out the front door in the last hour." Connor turned his piercing gaze on Elaine and Joe. "You were here first. Footprints in the snow on the steps?"

The two patrol officers looked at each other blankly.

"I'm not sure," Elaine said at last, and Joe shook his head.

"Sorry, Captain. The call came in originally as an unattended death. When we got here, I'm afraid we didn't worry about footprints on the walk."

Connor raised his hands in a helpless gesture. "Well, I'm banking on the shooter coming in the front door and leaving the same way."

A technician arrived to take more pictures, and it wasn't long before the hearse came for the body. The family was gone by then. Neil and Joe made the rounds downstairs, checking every window and door, finding no obvious point of entry. They went into the cellar, and Neil discovered that the bulkhead door was locked and the new snow outside undisturbed. Upstairs they found one window unlocked. Neil looked out critically and decided no one had left via that exit. The snow on the back porch roof below was melting, but signs of a human's going out that way would still be visible.

They went to report to Connor in the living room.

"Strange," said Connor. "Two old people alone in a house. No sign of an outsider coming in here, yet she's been shot. No weapon. He says he had none."

"You think he did it and stashed the gun?" Neil asked.

"Where?"

Neil shrugged.

"You, Elaine and Joe go over this room again, please. Look for something beyond the obvious. I suppose you checked the fireplace?"

"Yes, sir, but we'll check it again," said Elaine.

They continued searching the house. Looking out a dining room window, Neil noted that Kate's red compact car was still parked out front. When he turned, Connor was entering the room.

"Why is Kate sitting out front?" Neil asked.

Connor winced. "I should have told her not to come."

Neil peered down across the sloping lawn at the car, but from that angle, he couldn't see the driver.

"She wants to write the story for the *Press Herald*," Connor said.

Neil stared at him. "She's working at the paper now?"

Connor waved one hand in the air. "I know, I know. Conflict of interest and all that. It's not like I told her about the murder. She heard me when I told Adri why I wouldn't be home for

Christmas dinner. I told you she'd moved to Portland and started working at the paper a few weeks ago."

"No. No, you never mentioned it. If you had, I would certainly remember that."

"Oh." Connor gave a contrite shrug. "Sorry. Well, she's on call for the paper today, and she said if I didn't let her tag along, she'd just follow me anyway, like any good reporter who accidentally heard a hot tip."

"That sounds like Kate." Neil recalled how Kate could dig her heels in during a disagreement. Still, he wondered how many of the officers working under the captain would have stood up to him like that.

"I'm afraid she's going to have a long wait today."

"You're going to brief her, though?"

"I guess I'll have to." Connor sighed. "I don't like giving an exclusive to a relative."

"Maybe some other newspeople will hear about it on the scanner and show up before you tell her, and you can hold a press conference. Then it won't look like nepotism."

"Possible. But it is Christmas Day." Connor's face brightened. "Hey, maybe I'll just make *you* do a press conference."

"Oh, no." Neil was pretty sure Connor was joking, but the slim chance he wasn't made him nervous. "I just can't believe you didn't tell me she'd moved to Portland."

"To be honest, Adri and I weren't sure how you'd react, so we put off telling you. Let's take a look outside," said Connor.

They went through the kitchen and out the back door. Neil was still mulling over his friend's actions. At least Connor could have warned him about Kate. The snow on the back steps and the lawn beyond lay in pristine splendor.

"Nobody came in or out this way," Connor said. He stepped down into the snow and Neil followed, though it meant getting his shoes wet. On each side of the porch, shrubs draped in snow hugged the house, and dead flower stalks thrust up out of the white expanse.

Neil looked up at the windows above the porch. "That's the window that was unlocked, but I'm sure no one stepped on the roof up there."

Connor considered the position of the window, the porch roof and the nearest tree. He shook his head. "No way."

Neil thought about it and looked all around. "So, Mrs. Riley must have opened the door and let him in."

Connor inhaled deeply. "Either that or the professor did it and is lying through his teeth."

"I don't buy that," Neil said.

"Me, either. There's the little question of the disappearing weapon. Pete Downey searched Riley's luggage and stayed with him while he packed his clothes. There's no way Gerald Riley took a gun out of this house."

"He could have stashed it before Elaine and Joe got here."

"Very slim chance, but where?"

Neil shrugged. "We've got to keep looking."

Connor nodded. "That's part of your job this afternoon. And if someone came in from outside, he arrived and left again between 8:40 and 8:55 this morning. Did he come here on foot?"

Neil followed his reasoning. "So we ask all the neighbors if a car was parked along the street this morning. Also, if they saw anyone walking in the area."

"Excuse me. Connor?"

Neil and Connor whirled around. Kate stood at the edge of the lawn in a red wool coat and high-topped boots. Her deep chestnut hair waved about her rosy cheeks. Neil looked into her deep blue eyes, and his mouth went dry. Why had he been such an idiot last summer? He shot a glance at Connor.

"Hey, Kate, I thought I asked you to wait in the car," Connor said.

"Sorry. I just wondered if you could throw me a bone so I can keep my editor happy. He's threatened to call in a more experienced reporter, and I'd hate to lose my first chance at a big story."

"Sure." Connor sighed and glanced at his watch. "Listen, I've got to check in at the police station. There's no way I'm going to make it home for dinner. Could you call Adri and tell her?"

"I just talked to her. She says she and Mom have everything under control, and we'll have the big dinner this evening. Whenever you can be there."

"Thanks."

Kate looked deliberately at Neil. "Hi, Neil."

"Hi."

Ten yards of four-inch-deep snow separated them. For a second, Neil wished they were closer; then he wished they were miles apart. Could they ever feel comfortable in the same universe again? He turned to Connor. "Hey, there's a deli a couple of blocks from here. Why don't you and Kate run over and see if they're open? Get a sandwich and give her enough to start her story with."

Connor's phone rang again and he pulled it out with a sigh as he answered it. "Yeah? Can't it wait?" He shook his head slightly. "Okay, I'll be there in a little while." He stuffed the phone back in his pocket and turned to Neil. "I've got to go back to the office. Sergeant Legere needs me for a few minutes. How about *you* take Kate for a bite and bring her up to speed?"

"Well…" Neil's pulse kicked up a notch, and he zipped another glance at Kate. Throwing him and Kate together was the last thing he'd expected from Connor. "Sure, if Kate doesn't mind."

She eyed him cautiously. "Sure. You can tell me about the murder, and…maybe we can clear the air on a few other things."

Neil swallowed hard.

Connor nodded. "You can give her the basics. Nothing sensitive. You understand. And when you come back, you, Joe and Elaine tear this house apart. Figuratively speaking, of course." He turned toward Kate. "Neil will know what information we can let you publish. If there's anything new this afternoon, I'll brief you when I get home."

"Really? Thanks."

Suddenly Neil wanted to be with Kate again, up close, looking into those vivid blue eyes. But that could never happen. Could it? The last time he'd seen her, she'd made it clear she didn't want to see him again, and he didn't really blame her. But things had changed. She must recognize that, too, or she wouldn't consent to letting him brief her on the case. In that moment, Neil knew he wanted to straighten things out with her. Could he possibly wangle an invitation at the Larson house tonight?

Remorse struck him. He hadn't even called his mother to let her know his presence at the traditional dinner at one o'clock was out of the question. He couldn't duck out on leftover roast beef tonight at his parents' house, too. Not even for a chance to make things right with Kate. But would their impromptu lunch give them time enough to really talk?

"Neil!"

He jumped. "Yeah?"

Connor scowled at him. "I said, send Elaine and Joe for a lunch when you come back. I'll be gone an hour or so."

"Right." Neil looked over at Kate. "I'll come through the house and meet you out front."

She nodded and started walking around the corner of the house.

Neil realized Connor was watching him.

"You sure you're all right with that? Lunch with Kate, I mean?"

"Yeah. I guess."

Connor's brows drew together. "Maybe I shouldn't have suggested it. If I weren't so swamped—"

"It's okay." Neil smiled and tried to believe it.

Connor glanced at his watch again. "Okay, about that missing weapon."

"Yeah?" Neil asked.

"I can only think of one thing Riley could have done with it, short of stashing it in the house."

"What's that?" It came to Neil in a flash, and he looked up at the window again. "You think he threw it out the window?"

Connor shrugged. "I don't, really, but it was the only thing that was unlocked. You'd better examine this area." He waved his arm to encompass the back lawn. Dozens of divots in the snow showed where melting clumps had fallen from the branches of the one big maple tree in the yard. Any one of them could have been made by a thrown object. "Keep on with the house search, and start questioning the neighbors."

"Right," said Neil. "But we'll need more men. And metal detectors."

TWO

Kate unwrapped her sandwich as she faced Neil across a small table in the deli. Now, on her first opportunity in months to study him up close, she gave the detective mixed marks. He was still handsome, all right. Dark, wavy hair and chocolate-brown eyes, the hint of a dimple on his firm jaw. But his attractive appearance wasn't all good in her book. She wanted—needed—a professional relationship with her sources in the police department. She didn't want to be distracted by his good looks or her own stray thoughts of what had happened between them last summer. She shut down that train of thought in a hurry. This was her big story. Period.

"So, Connor is requisitioning more uniformed officers for the investigation?"

"Right," Neil said. "He and I were the only two detectives available this morning. Christmas is putting a cramp in our usual style of investigating a homicide. We'll be using patrolmen to help us canvass the neighborhood and take statements. Someone may have seen something this morning that will help us."

Kate nodded. Neil was acting professional, and so could she. Still, it would have been much easier if Connor had given her the information she needed himself. "I really appreciate this, Neil. I'm at the bottom of the journalistic ladder, and this story could mean a big boost to my career. But I've never covered a criminal case before, so treat me like the most ignorant person you've ever seen. No detail is too obvious for me."

He laughed nervously, and she took a bite of her sandwich, deliberately not looking at him.

"Well, I'm happy I can help," he said. "You have to understand that I can't tell you everything about the investigation, just—"

"Oh, I understand perfectly. I'm The Press, and you have to go by the book as to what access you give me."

An awkward silence settled between them as they dug in to their sandwiches and chips.

"Look, this is kind of weird. If you'd rather not—"

"Kate, I'm sorry."

She stared at him.

Neil clamped his lips together, his cheeks flushed and his eyes forlorn. After a long moment of silence, he said quietly, "I mean it. I didn't treat you very well. Actually, I treated you horribly. I…I'm sorry." He blinked and crumpled up his napkin. "I've wanted to say that to you for a long time, but I figured you didn't want to hear from me, so I didn't try to contact you."

Kate reached for her glass of water and took a sip, easing it past the hot lump in her throat. She still didn't trust her voice.

Neil eyed her bleakly. "Connor and Adrienne didn't even tell me you'd moved to Portland."

She nodded. "I asked them not to."

His lips twitched. He leaned back in his chair and toyed with the napkin. At last he looked up at her. His brown eyes reflected the hurt she still felt.

"You haven't been coming to their church." It was little more than a whisper, but it struck home.

Kate bowed her head. "They told me you've been going with them, and I didn't want you to feel you had to stay away." He started to speak, but she held up one hand. "My apartment is on the other side of town, near the university. I've found a church over there. It's all right. Really."

He shook his head, frowning. "That doesn't seem right."

She inhaled carefully, choosing her words. "I know you're close to Connor. I don't want to interfere with your friendship. I've only been in town four weeks, and I've been really busy." She'd known that sooner or later she'd have to face Neil, but the move and her challenging new job had occupied her. Somehow she'd managed to avoid thinking about this moment.

"Okay," he said at last. "We can work together if we have to. I promise I won't get out of line."

She couldn't meet his gaze then. Hot tears hovered, only a blink away. How many nights had she cried herself to sleep after she broke up with Neil? She was certain Connor had raked him over the coals when he learned how deeply she'd been hurt.

But they'd moved on. They'd both grown up a little. She knew she was tougher now. And she would know better than to let herself fall in love with a man who'd dated half the female population of the city. According to her sister, Neil had come a long way. Good. But she didn't think she wanted to get too close to the white-hot stove that had burned her before.

"Kate?"

She nodded. "Sure. We're both adults. If I need to contact you for news, treat me like you would any other reporter. I don't expect any special favors, from Connor or from you."

"Okay. We'll stick to business."

"Great." Somehow, that didn't make her feel better. She reached for the last bite of her sandwich. Connor was Neil's boss, and he still considered Neil his friend, even after Kate's short-lived relationship with Neil and the painful blowup when it ended. She knew they'd had words, but the rift had healed. Apparently Neil had started attending church shortly afterward and had made a profession of faith. They seemed to work well together, and Connor trusted Neil to be in charge of the investigation while he tended to his other duties. Would he think so highly of Neil if he hadn't truly changed? She would watch and wait before she decided how she felt about Neil now.

She opened her notebook and clicked her pen. "So…who was the victim? Professor Riley or his wife?"

Neil stopped chewing and stared at her a moment before swallowing. "How did you know the home owner's name?"

"I looked up the address on my laptop. That house was featured in a garden club tour in July. Mrs. Riley's an active member of the club and a green thumb extraordinaire. Her flower beds must be something when they're not buried in snow."

"I'm impressed. Have you thought about going into law enforcement?"

"Not really. I love to write. But I do love puzzles, too."

"Mmm. Well, this is one I hope we can solve." Neil took another bite of his sandwich.

After swallowing, he told her, "The victim is Edna Riley, age sixty-eight. Her body was discovered this morning by her husband. You already know his name, though."

"I do."

"Well, the medical examiner who responded was Dr. Jacob McIntyre. We'll be getting a full autopsy report from him in a few days."

Kate wrote as fast as she could, saddened that a woman's life had been taken yet energized as she conducted her first major interview. This was exactly the way she had pictured her life as a reporter.

By sundown, Neil's stomach was rumbling. The sandwich he'd had with Kate at the deli was only a distant memory. He tried not to imagine all the delights he had missed at his mother's Christmas dinner table. One thing she had made clear when he called her—if he didn't show up by 7:00 p.m., he would regret it. What that meant, Neil wasn't exactly sure. Maybe she would return his Christmas gifts for refunds. Or maybe she would disinherit him and leave everything to his sisters, Anneke and Marianne. They had married and provided his mother with grandchildren, as she always reminded him that good children should. Well, if he ever found the woman God wanted him to spend the rest of his life with, maybe he would, too. Until then he believed he was making a difference with his work, helping people. He'd stay focused on that and do the best job he could.

After lunch, Kate had left and Neil headed back to the crime scene. More uniformed officers arrived, and Connor returned from his trip to the police station. By five o'clock, the Rileys' entire yard was trampled and gone over with metal detectors, and every inch of the house had been inspected. No gun. No anything.

The captain sent all the patrolmen home. As he and Neil walked to their vehicles, Connor took out his cell phone, called Adrienne and told her to expect him and Neil in an hour.

Neil was tempted, but only for a moment. Although he was still attracted to Kate—his racing pulse when they'd met this morning proved that—he figured they'd about said it all during lunch. She didn't want to be around him unless it was work related. Since receiving Christ a few months before, Neil had gotten off the dating merry-go-round. Before, it was just a game. Now, he realized how many women he had hurt. Women like Kate, who had hoped for a serious relationship when he just wanted to have a good time. Before, he hadn't taken her faith seriously. Big mistake. He knew she'd been right to break it off before things got out of hand. Now he wasn't sure how to act around a Christian woman, and he didn't want to mess things up again. Better just to leave the past in the past.

He looked at Connor. "My mother will kill me if I don't show up at home. I'm sorry."

Connor shrugged. "It's okay."

"Well, you know. It's not Dutch to miss Christmas dinner. Mama won't accept any excuses tonight."

"All right. How did lunch go? I wondered after I left if that was such a good idea."

Neil paused beside the door of his pickup. "It was okay. We needed to talk. There were things that needed to be said. We managed to keep it civil."

"Good." Connor stepped away. "Go see your folks. Come over later if you feel like it. We'll save you some pie."

"All right," Neil said. "You want me to go log the evidence?"

"Sure. I'm going to stop by the hotel and see Mr. Riley for a minute."

Neil left him and drove to the police station, mulling over the day's events. He was still learning to communicate with God and with his family, where he sometimes felt like a misfit. How could he expect to get along with someone like Kate, who had seen him at his worst?

He pulled into the police station parking lot and shut the engine off, then leaned back and closed his eyes. *Lord, I'm not ready to start a social relationship in the Christian world—or overhaul an old one. Am I? I don't know how to act around Kate. I want to do what's right.* As he gathered the bags of evidence they'd collected at the Riley house and walked into the station, he still wasn't sure whether he would accept Connor's invitation.

Kate clicked Send on the e-mail message and reached for her cell phone.

"Darrin? I just sent you my first installment."

"Great. It's coming in now."

"But Captain Larson is going to update me again soon. Do you want me to write a separate article, or just send some more copy you can add onto this one?"

"Uh…better ask the night editor. Jan just came in, and I'll be leaving soon, so you need to talk to her. Oh, and I swapped with Stephanie, so I have New Year's Eve off. Thanks! Hold on."

Kate sighed and leaned back on the bed. Adrienne and Connor's guest room was much more comfortable than her room in/the apartment she shared with two University of Southern Maine coeds. Maybe she should take her sister up on her offer to move in with them. She'd turned them down initially because she wanted to strike out on her own. But a month of rooming with Salli and Madyson had somewhat jaded her on independence. It was too much like her own college days. Loud music, strange young men visiting, and the girls giggling and partying and coming in late. Kate longed for the stability she saw in her sister's home. Maybe it was time to ask Adrienne if she could reconsider.

She could picture just how she would set up the room. Her

computer desk on the wall beside the door, her stereo and book-shelf to the left...

"Jan Etchison."

Kate sat up. "Hi, Jan. This is Kate Richards."

"Who?"

"Kate Richards. We haven't met. I've been with the *Press Herald* about a month."

"Oh, are you the intern from the university?"

"No." Kate felt her cheeks color, which was ridiculous. The editor couldn't even see her. "I'm a full-time reporter. I'm on call today, and there's a big story breaking."

"Darrin said you had something about a homicide, that right?"

"Yes."

"He's sending the story to my computer. Just a sec."

Kate exhaled and waited, her stomach doing little walkovers. She wasn't sure if it was nerves or because she hadn't eaten anything since the sandwich at the deli with Neil five hours ago. She'd sweated all of Christmas afternoon over her story, telling herself an enormous turkey dinner would be her reward.

"Okay, I'm looking at it," Jan said. "Oh, you connected with Connor Larson?"

"Uh...yeah, I did."

"He's really good with our reporters. He'll walk you through all the evidence."

"Yeah, he and his top detective pretty much did that, and the captain's promised to give me more tonight. I don't think anyone else is on this story yet. It's like...an exclusive." She flinched, wondering if she should have used the E-word.

"Looks pretty good," Jan said. "We'll put this on the Web right away. Tell you what, if you talk to Larson again by nine, call me. We'll update the lead. Let me see how much space we've got tonight.... Okay, I'd say you could add another ten inches, no more. Page one, and jump to A-eight."

Kate exhaled, grinning from ear to ear. "Thanks! I'll be in touch." She hung up and sat still for a moment. Suddenly, she pumped her fists in the air. "Yes! Page one. Thank you, Lord." Then she sobered and bowed her head as she thought of poor Professor Riley and his family spending Christmas in a hotel, mourning the sudden loss of Mrs. Riley.

"Lord, please comfort Professor Riley and his family today. Please let the killer be caught and brought to justice, and if You can use me to help in that process in any way, I'm all Yours."

She jumped up and opened the closet. Time she spiffed up a little and offered to help her sister in the kitchen.

Ten minutes later, she went down the stairs. Her father and younger brother, Travis, sat in the living room watching a football game. On her father's lap sat Matthew, Adrienne and Connor's three-year-old son.

"About time you put in an appearance," her father said.

"Sorry. I've been busy."

He smiled as she stooped to hug him. "We're proud of you, honey."

"Thanks." Kate ambled through the sunroom into Adrienne's kitchen. Her mom and Adrienne, wearing bib aprons, were dashing about preparing food.

"No, not that dish, Mom. Use the blue one. And the potato masher is in that drawer."

"Hey, Adri. What can I do to help?" Kate asked.

Adrienne's blue eyes lit at her greeting. "Hi, Kate! Done with your article?"

"For now. Connor said he'll give me some more information when he comes home."

"Well, that will be any minute now. He called a little while ago, and he's bringing his buddy."

Kate paused and took a deep breath. "I don't suppose that would be the high-power detective I had lunch with?"

"Depends. Was he a cute Dutchman, a little taller than Connor, with chocolate-brown eyes and a hundred-watt smile?"

"Well, I suppose. I was thinking more about the scoop he tossed my way than about his smile." She threw Adrienne a weak smile and walked to the sink to wash her hands.

"You had lunch with Neil?" Adrienne handed her an apron. "How did that happen?"

"Connor got called away, so Neil briefed me for my story on the murder."

Adrienne's jaw dropped. "And it went okay?"

"Yes, we both lived through it." Kate took the apron and shook it out.

Her mother turned from where she was mashing potatoes at the counter. "That's not like Connor to go off and leave you two alone. Doesn't he know how you feel about Neil?"

"I'm sure he does." Kate shrugged. "Mom, it was a long time ago."

"Not that long."

"Long enough. Neil and I are both mature enough to work together in spite of the past."

Her mother frowned at her. "You make it sound like nothing. You were devastated six months ago."

Kate took a moment to settle her thoughts and breathe a silent prayer for a calm spirit. "You're right, Mom, but you know what Adrienne and Connor have been telling us—Neil is a Christian now. I was a little leery of him, but he was very polite today, and—" she glanced at Adrienne "—and he apologized."

Adrienne's sunny smile broke out, but their mother said, "Humph. We'll see how he behaves. You're not going out with him again, are you?"

"No," Kate said. "I'm going to get my career started and my byline established before I start thinking about romance." She stretched to tie the apron strings behind her back.

"But you ate lunch with him," her mother said.

"Mom, it was just a sandwich. And he gave me a page-one story."

"Know what? I'm glad you two ran into each other and got it over with." Adrienne rubbed her stomach and arched her back.

"You'd better get off your feet, Adri." Her mother swept past her with a dish of sweet pickles in one hand and a butter dish in the other.

"How's my little niece or nephew doing?" Kate asked.

"Active," Adrienne said, kneading her side. "Very active."

Kate saw the flash of headlights come through the window and the reflection on the wall and walked to the door that led to the breezeway. She peeked out through the glass. "Connor's home."

"Great! Let's get the veggies on," Adrienne said. "Mom, will you ask Dad to come take the turkey out of the oven?"

Kate managed to contain her anticipation over more details for her story until Connor had kissed Adrienne, tossed Matthew in the air and greeted his in-laws.

"Where's Neil?" Adrienne asked.

"Oh, he had to go to his parents' for dinner. Sorry. He'll try to come over later for dessert." He smiled down at Adrienne. "Give me a minute and let me lose this necktie, okay?" As he headed toward the master bedroom, he peeled off his blazer and reached to unbuckle his shoulder holster.

"Uh, Connor? Got a sec?"

He turned with a wary smile. "Sure, Kate. What do you need to know?"

"Anything you can tell me. I handed in what I wrote up this afternoon, but if I can add a few more inches, it'd be great."

"I may as well tell you, Channels 8 and 13 showed up this afternoon."

"Oh." Kate swallowed her disappointment. The local television news broadcasters would break the story tonight, and her report wouldn't see print until tomorrow morning. "Well, the paper is putting it on its Web site today, anyway. A lot of people read that."

He flashed her a smile. "Good point. Well, here's some detail you can put in the paper that no one else knows yet. I visited Mr. Riley again, and he was adamant he didn't see or hear anything unusual this morning. As far as he knows, no one came to the house. He admits he's hard of hearing, but he said he usually hears the doorbell. He didn't hear it ring this morning before he found his wife's body."

"That means he didn't hear any gunshots, either?"

"No, but if his hearing's not very good, and it was a single shot from a small-caliber pistol…" Connor shook his head in dismissal. "A silencer could have been used, but I doubt it."

"What about that upstairs window?" Kate asked.

He frowned. "Did Neil tell you about that?"

She shrugged. "No, he didn't mention it. But this morning I saw the two of you looking up at it and talking."

"Yeah, well…did you put that in your story?"

She shook her head. "I didn't think you would want me to. But I keep thinking about it."

"Thanks. We don't want the killer to read the paper and know everything we know."

"Right."

Connor loosened the knot in his necktie. "Well, Mr. Riley said it was probably just an oversight that one window wasn't locked, and we didn't find any evidence that anyone had gone in or out the window, or thrown anything out of it. So I don't think it's important to the case."

"Okay. Do you get a lot of false clues like that?"

"Sometimes. And we have to follow every lead."

"Sure. Anything else?"

"Well, both Mr. Riley and his son, William, claim they don't own any guns."

"They could be lying."

Connor grimaced. "The old man seemed genuine. And the son can prove he was on the road with his family at the time of the murder."

"So…he has an alibi. Do you have any other suspects?"

"Well, that's a loaded question. If I say no, people will think the police department is incompetent. But if I say yes, the press will hound me to know who I'm looking at."

"I won't hound you, Connor."

"No?" He laughed. "Let me go change my shirt, will you, Kate?"

"Oh, sure. Sorry."

He went into the bedroom and closed the door. She realized he had evaded her question.

Over the dinner table, Neil's name came up again.

"Maybe we'll get to meet him at last," Kate's mother said. "But I'm not sure I want to."

"I know Neil and Kate had their differences last summer," Connor said, "but I think they're past that. Neil is my best detective. He's smart, which is what's important when it comes to detective work."

Adrienne laughed. "He's very sweet, too, and he's cute."

"How can a guy like that do undercover work?" Kate asked.

"What do you mean?" Connor asked.

"Oh, come on. He'd turn heads anywhere."

Adrienne stared at her with wide eyes, but Kate shrugged. Just because she admitted she still found Neil attractive didn't mean she was about to lose her heart again.

"That's a drawback in some situations," Connor admitted. "But Neil doesn't do a lot of undercover work. He's more of an investigator. And he's a charmer, which is a plus. Women will tell him anything." He winked at Kate, and she feared her cheeks were turning red.

Her mother said, "Adrienne told me once that he's broken more hearts than he can count."

"He did break a few, once upon a time, but he's changed in the last few months. A lot." Connor passed his father-in-law the dish of squash.

"What do you mean?" Mrs. Richards asked.

"Didn't Adrienne tell you that Neil became a Christian a few months ago?"

"She mentioned it."

"It was in August, I think." Connor picked up his fork. "He's still rough around the edges, but he's growing." He took a bite of turkey and chewed.

"And he's a good cop," Kate mused.

"Neil has always had a terrific work ethic. I was responsible for his training when he first came into the Priority Unit three years ago. I never saw anyone take to it so fast. But he was a little wild, I don't deny that. I see a big difference in his personal life since he was saved, though. He's a lot steadier, more dependable."

"Fewer broken hearts?" Mr. Richards asked with a smile.

Connor shrugged. "He hasn't had a steady girl that I know of since Kate sent him packing. He's my best friend now, and I'm proud to say that."

Kate could feel her parents staring at her. She asked Connor, "How does that work, with you being his boss?"

"The fact that I was promoted doesn't bother our friendship. I do have to be careful to treat Neil the same as I do all the men in my unit when we're working, that's all."

Kate hoped the change was as genuine as Connor claimed. And she hoped her parents would treat Neil civilly if he visited. Now that she'd seen him again, she knew she could forgive him for the pain he'd caused her. No sense in her parents holding a grudge.

An hour later, Neil arrived. Adrienne let him into the kitchen, where she and Kate had just finished loading the dishwasher.

"Hello, Neil, I'm glad you could come. I understand you and Kate had lunch together today."

Neil shot Kate a smile that she could only construe as shy, which startled her. When they'd first met, he'd come on strong. She'd heard he was anything but timid with women, but she'd been so attracted to him, she hadn't cared at the time.

"Yes, I enjoyed it," he said.

She smiled at him, determined not to let his good looks and charm sway her again. "Nice to see you again, Neil."

He turned the wattage up then, and she had to look away. In spite of her resolve, her pulse hammered a quiet tattoo. Right now she didn't need that type of distraction. Her plan was to hone her craft, outshine the other reporters she worked with, garner a few writing awards and secure her place as a top-notch journalist. Maybe then she'd have time to consider having a personal life. But it wouldn't be with Connor's reformed bad boy, handsome though he might be. She wanted someone stable when the time came.

They all settled down in the living room, and Kate and her mother served the pies, insisting that Adrienne sit beside Connor and put her feet up. They brought the last plates in, and Kate handed one to her brother, Travis, keeping one for herself. When she looked around for a seat, the only chair vacant was next to Neil's.

She sat down gingerly, throwing him a sideways glance.

"Do you like it at the paper?" he asked.

"I love it, but it's a challenge."

He nodded and took a bite of his pecan pie.

Kate took a few bites and tried to focus on the rest of the family, not just Neil, but she couldn't stop being aware of him.

Her father didn't help matters. He drew everyone's attention to Neil by saying, "I understand you and Connor are good friends now."

Neil swallowed quickly. "That's right, sir. When I passed the detective's exam a few years ago, Connor was the senior detective in our unit. He had to train me and watch my back. I guess I gave him a lot of headaches when I first came into the unit."

"That's an understatement," Connor said, and everyone laughed. "But after a while, I realized Neil wasn't just a hard-headed kid. He's a good cop."

Neil smiled and looked anywhere but at his captain. "Well, I've learned a lot from Connor these past few years."

Connor laid his plate and fork on the end table. "Let me brief you on what happened after we left the Riley house, Neil."

He rose and Neil followed him toward the study. Kate felt a pang of disappointment. He was going to tell Neil things he wouldn't tell her, because she was a reporter. He didn't trust her. He would tell Adrienne everything later, when they were alone, but he wouldn't tell his sister-in-law, the wet-behind-the-ears reporter who might spill something sensitive. She put the last bite of pie into her mouth.

At the study door, Connor let Neil precede him out of the

room, then turned and looked directly at her. "Hey, Kate, you want in on this?"

She jumped to her feet, dropping her napkin. "You mean it?"

Connor jerked his head toward the study door. She hurried toward him. Her mother intercepted her and snatched her dishes from her hand.

They entered the study, and Connor closed the door behind the three of them. He and Adrienne had turned the house's formal dining room into an office. Both had computer desks. File cabinets, bookshelves, a fax machine and a serious-looking copier rounded out the furnishings.

Connor nodded toward the chair at Adrienne's desk. "Have a seat."

He pulled another chair out from the wall for Neil and swiveled his own desk chair and sat down. "All right, so I posted a patrolman at the scene. They'll cover the site until we go back tomorrow."

Neil nodded. "I logged all the evidence in. Did you talk to the Rileys?"

"Yes. They'll stay at the hotel tonight and head down to Dover in the morning. William said they would keep his father there a couple of days and then bring him home before the funeral. He gave me the contact information, and I assured the elder Mr. Riley his house will be guarded until he comes back."

Kate watched them, in awe of their professional manner. Both men were confident and well established in their careers. She, on the other hand, was the small-town girl trying to make good in the city. Her year at the weekly paper two hours to the north didn't count for much in this game, and she needed to show that she could succeed in the big leagues. The prospect of failing in her chosen field scared her silly. She swallowed the lump of inadequacy that threatened to choke her. *Remember, girl, you're the one listening to these two brilliant detectives discuss their case. Connor trusts you enough to let you write a story about his unit—one that could affect his reputation. So don't blow it.* She wished she had grabbed her notebook.

Connor had been a part of her family for four years now, and she'd gotten to know him fairly well. The three weeks she'd spent with him and Adrienne in June, when she'd met Neil, had strained the family tie. She regretted that. Suddenly, his approval of her article was more important than her editor's.

"The preliminary report from the M.E. is a single gunshot wound to the chest," Connor said. "He'll remove the bullet in the autopsy Monday, and we'll get it so we can run ballistics."

"Great," Neil said. "What are we doing tomorrow?"

"We'll collect all the keys and do more interviews in the neighborhood. I don't want to work all day Sunday, but we can't let people's memories get cold."

"So what does all this mean?" Kate dared to ask. "Can you tell me your overall impression of the case at this moment?"

Connor leaned back in his chair. "If Mr. Riley killed his wife, he had to ditch the weapon. So far we don't see how he could have done that. The evidence points to someone entering the house with a gun this morning, killing Mrs. Riley and taking the weapon with him when he left. We've established that it wasn't a robbery. Nothing was taken."

"Mr. Riley agrees," Neil said.

"A robber probably would have taken the Limoges figurines off the mantel in the living room," said Connor.

Neil's brow furrowed. "Maybe it was a foiled burglary attempt and he was interrupted right after he shot her. Heard her husband coming down the stairs and ran away without taking anything."

"No," said Connor. "In that case, he'd have gone out the front door or a window, but everything was locked downstairs. The person with the gun either didn't leave the house or stopped long enough to lock the dead bolt on that front door with a key. So he didn't dash off in a hurry."

"Did you ask Riley about his wife's health?" Neil asked.

"I did. He said she had a little arthritis, but she was in good health for her age. We can check her medical records, but his son corroborated his story. No chronic health problems."

"Can I print that?" Kate asked. "That she's believed to have been in good health, I mean? Because you hear stories about people killing a loved one who is terminally ill."

"Sure, I don't see any harm in putting that question to rest."

It was a tiny fragment, but slowly she was gathering bits that would round out her story and make it a good article, not merely an adequate account of the crime.

Connor stood up. The lines at the corners of his eyes looked deeper than usual. "I told the family they can enter the house in the morning if they wish, before they go to Dover, but not to enter the rooms we taped off. Mr. Riley may want to get some more clothes or something."

"So…that's it?" Kate asked.

He shrugged. "I can give you the name of the funeral home. I think the son was helping Mr. Riley prepare the obituary. They were talking about holding a memorial service after the body is released, but that won't be until next week sometime."

"Thanks, Connor. If you'll excuse me, I think I'll go type up the things we've talked about tonight. There's just enough time for me to do that before my deadline. You don't mind, do you?"

"Go for it."

She stood, and Neil rose, too. He spoke as she moved toward the door.

"Good luck, Kate. Everyone in southern Maine will be reading your words in the morning."

She caught her breath and looked back at him. "That's a little scary."

The irresistible smile flashed. "You'll do great."

Kate hurried up to the guest room and her laptop wanting desperately to believe him.

THREE

After Kate left the room, Neil sensed that Connor was watching him.

"What?"

"If you treat her badly again, I'll kill you."

Neil stared at him, at a loss. "I don't think you need to worry about that. Kate isn't interested in dating me anymore."

"But you're still interested in her?"

"Well…" Neil hesitated.

"Kate is family. Do you know how upset Adrienne would be if you hurt her sister again?"

"Oh, come on, Con. You know I'm not like that anymore. I haven't had a relationship in months, and I'm not planning on one now."

Connor shook his head. "I'm sorry. I'd trust you with my life, but this…"

"I was an idiot," Neil said. "I didn't realize what a wonderful woman Kate is until it was too late. If it's any consolation, she was right to break it off."

"You're telling me?" Connor bristled, and Neil wished he could just change the subject. Reminders of his wild past made him feel terrible, but he knew that to keep Connor's newly earned respect, he had to accept his friend's judgment.

"I don't blame you for not telling me she was back in town. But I mean it, Connor. I'm through dating until I learn how to go about it the right way."

Connor nodded slowly. "Okay. But I'm serious. If Adrienne's

sister sheds even one tear over you, I'll break every bone in your body."

"Got it." Neil thought of protesting further, but maybe it was better to let actions speak louder than words. It could take a long time for people to trust him in this area.

Connor nodded and slapped him on the back. "Great. Let's get some coffee. And I think our gift to you is still under the tree."

"Oh, I've got a little something for you and Adrienne out in my truck, too."

Neil went out to the driveway and retrieved the package. Light snow was falling. When he went back inside, he wiped his shoes on the mat and went into the living room.

"You folks aren't heading to Skowhegan tonight, are you?" he asked Kate and Adrienne's father, Bob Richards.

"No, the kids are putting us up here tonight."

"Good," Neil said. "It's snowing. The interstate will probably be a little slick." He walked over to the sofa and placed the gift in Adrienne's hands. "Here, Adri. Just a little something for you guys."

She smiled. "Thank you, Neil. We have something for you, too."

Connor held out a small wrapped package.

"Thanks." Neil sat down and removed the wrapping paper carefully. The entire family—minus Kate—watched him. In the box was a compact, leather-covered Bible. He lifted it out, unsnapped the cover and riffled the pages. He smiled at Adrienne. "New car smell."

She laughed. "You like it?"

"Yeah, it's terrific. Small enough to carry everywhere. Thanks."

"Did your family open their gifts today?" Adrienne's mother, Marilyn, asked.

"No, actually we did it on Sinterklaas."

Mrs. Richards smiled blankly.

"It's...um...St. Nicholas' Eve," he said. "December fifth. The Dutch people celebrate then."

"How interesting! But they do celebrate Christmas Day, too?"

"Oh, yes. It's a big occasion."

Adrienne pulled the wrapping paper off the present he'd given her. "Oh, too bad we put Matthew to bed. He'll love this." She took out a collection of stuffed nativity figures one by one and set them up on the coffee table.

"Oh, how sweet," said Mrs. Richards.

"That's nice, Neil," Connor said. "My mother had a set she used to put out every year, too, only it was china. She used to let me set it up. I broke the donkey's leg once, and my dad had to glue it."

"Well, the kids won't be able to break this one." Adrienne picked up the Mary figure. "All hand-stitched, I'd say. Beautiful detail."

"I thought maybe Matthew and the new little one could play with it at Christmastime." Neil couldn't help smiling. He sat back, content. Why couldn't his own family be as calm and restful as this one? He'd thought his mother would scalp him when he left the family gathering after a scant two hours. But his mother's nagging, the inane chatter, the noisy nieces and nephews running wild through the house and his inebriated brother-in-law telling jokes that weren't funny… No, he didn't miss being at his family's Christmas celebration.

He looked around just in time to see Kate coming down the stairs again. She met his gaze and smiled. He had to admit Kate made his Christmas a whole lot brighter.

Connor picked Neil up at his apartment at seven-thirty the next morning.

"You didn't tell me the elevator was broken again," he said when Neil opened the door.

"Sorry. You could have just called me and told me you were parked out front."

"True. You ready? I just want to check in at the office before church."

Neil pulled his winter jacket on over his dress shirt and tie, and the two men headed for the station.

A stack of crime scene photos and officers' reports waited on Connor's desk. The captain sat down and started reading, and Neil looked at the pictures. As Connor laid each sheet aside, Neil picked it up and read it. He knew it wouldn't bother Connor; he'd done that for years on cases they'd worked together.

At last Connor sat back in his chair, waiting for Neil to read the last report. "Doesn't add up," he said, shaking his head.

"He had to come in the front door," Neil said. "And leave by it."

"Yeah. Too bad the first responders didn't think about footprints."

Neil shrugged. "I suppose I might have found something when I got there, but four cops had already been in and out. To be frank, I knew they were inside, and I didn't think about messing up the prints on the front steps."

"I know. It's not your fault. If the uniforms had known it was a homicide…Well, no use fretting about that. The killer used either the front door or no door at all."

"You mean Mr. Riley."

"Can't conclusively rule him out yet."

Neil said, "No gunshot residue on his hands."

"Yeah. I guess he's out of it. I just keep coming back to him because we don't have anyone else, you know?" Connor sighed and stacked the reports, stuck them into a file folder and wrote "Riley" on the tab.

Neil said, "If the shooter left by the front door, he must have had a key to lock the door behind him. Mr. Riley said he found the door still locked. So we need to know who had keys."

"Right. And also who benefits from Mrs. Riley's death. Call the hotel, would you?" Connor turned on his computer.

Neil called the hotel where William Riley had taken his father.

"They checked out," he told Connor.

The captain called the officer on duty at Gerald Riley's house and learned the family had not appeared there that morning.

"They must be on the road to New Hampshire," Connor said. "We might as well go to church."

Neil nodded. "We can call Dover later and see if they got home safely. And tomorrow we'll find out if there was a will, and who had keys to the house."

Kate was a little nervous about going into the singles' Sunday school class of Connor and Adrienne's church. Her sister had persuaded her to meet them there, now that the trauma of seeing Neil was past. Kate wondered if she would like it and where she would fit in here. She might want to make this her new home church. She'd decided that if she wanted the total experience, she should dive in, so she left Adrienne in the vestibule and wandered into the classroom. The ratio of women to men was about eight to one. Coffee and pastries seemed the first order of the day.

She accepted a cup of black coffee and found a seat at the back of the room, next to a plump, cheerful young woman who introduced herself as Valerie.

"Oh, you're Adrienne's sister," Valerie cried as they exchanged information. "I just love Adrienne!"

About five minutes after the lesson began, the door at the back of the classroom opened, and Neil Alexander slipped in. He met Kate's gaze and arched his eyebrows with a quizzical smile. She smiled back, realizing with a start that he was walking toward her and the empty chair on her other side. Valerie caught her eye and made a surreptitious fanning motion with her hand, indicating with the gesture that Neil was hot stuff. Kate did her best to keep a straight face and concentrate on what the speaker was saying. Even so, she couldn't resist sneaking an occasional peek at Neil. He had a small Bible open. Though he fumbled a little finding the references, he seemed determined to keep up. He even took out a notebook and jotted down a few notes. He caught her looking once, and Kate blushed to the roots of her hair. Yep, that smile would mesmerize any woman. She could almost hear Valerie's palpitations.

When the class was over, they headed out toward the auditorium. Kate was sure the church members would assume they were interested in each other, but there was no help for it.

"I saw your story in the paper this morning," Neil said. "Good job."

"Thanks. The wire service picked it up." She hated the flush she felt creeping up her cheeks. She didn't feel that way about Neil now. Why couldn't she appear cool and collected when he was near?

"Does that mean all the papers in Maine printed it?" he asked.

"Yes, and maybe all over the country. With my byline."

"Christmas Day murder. It'll sell a lot of papers."

"Yeah. My editor wants me to do a follow-up for tomorrow's paper. I'll be talking to some of Mrs. Riley's neighbors and garden club friends." Kate intended to see if she could get anything fresh out of Connor later that day, too. And on Monday, she hoped he would give her some fresh information on the case that would give her another front-page story.

"So, are you staying over with Connor and Adrienne for a while?" Neil asked.

"Yeah. My parents and my brother are leaving today, but Adrienne asked me to stay a few more days." She hesitated, then decided it couldn't hurt to get an outside opinion. "Actually, she'd like me to move in. With the baby coming soon, she's thinking I could help her out some. They've hired a woman to come in and vacuum and that sort of thing one day a week, but Adrienne gets tired."

"Sounds like it would be a good move for everybody if you lived with them," Neil said.

"Yeah, the more I think about it, the more I like the idea. I could do laundry and things like that. And Connor would feel better knowing someone else was there with Adri when he's out on those late-night jaunts you guys take."

Neil laughed. "Yeah, we have to work when the criminals do."

Kate reflected that she'd have to do better about keeping a curfew than she had during her whirlwind romance with Neil. She'd behaved badly herself during her summer visit and had worried Adrienne sick. Not everything was Neil's fault.

They reached the auditorium, but the Larsons' pew was full. Kate's parents sat beside Adrienne, and next to Connor was another couple. Travis was squeezed in beside his father, and Matthew was cuddled up next to his grandma Richards.

"Who's the couple beside Connor?" Kate whispered to Neil.

"Mike and Sharon Crowley. Mike's our boss."

Kate stared at him. "You mean that's the chief of police, sitting right there?"

Neil nodded. "He hasn't been a Christian for long. His wife has been praying for Mike for years. He was saved not long after me."

"I don't suppose Connor had anything to do with that?"

Neil smiled. "Connor doesn't go around shoving the gospel down people's throats, but when the moment is right, he has a way of showing a person how badly he needs Christ. Want to sit here?"

As they entered a pew two rows behind her family, the pianist began to play, and everyone quit talking. Kate couldn't help noticing the faint masculine scent of the man next to her. It reminded her of the evergreen forest at the back of her father's farm in Skowhegan. If she were a romantic... But she wasn't. Adrienne was the romantic sister. Kate was the practical, goal-oriented one. She'd made one major mistake in her life—Neil. She wouldn't make it again. She focused her attention on Pastor Robinson.

After church, Connor invited Neil home for dinner as if it were an every-week occurrence. Kate felt she'd had more than enough of Neil for one day, but she kept her thoughts to herself. Adrienne kept the meal simple so that the Richards family could get on the road for their two-hour drive early in the afternoon.

Kate hugged her parents and Travis goodbye, promising to go home for a weekend soon. After they had driven away, the house seemed very quiet.

"Want me to strip the beds for you?" Kate asked.

Adrienne shook her head. "Let's leave it until tomorrow. But I'd love it if you could start the dishwasher for me."

"I'll help," Neil offered. He started gathering dirty dishes and carrying them toward the counter. This simple act brought Kate's memories crashing down on her, reminding her of how sweet and irresistible he'd seemed last summer and how hard she'd fallen for him.

Okay, he's polite and not above helping with housework. That's not enough to base a relationship on. Not even with a way-too-handsome man.

"I think I'll call William Riley in Dover and make sure they got home all right," Connor said. A few minutes later, he came into the kitchen. Kate was watching Neil awkwardly load the silverware into the dishwasher. She forced herself not to show him how to do it right.

"The Rileys are doing okay," Connor said to Neil. "They plan to bring Gerald back up here in a couple of days. The funeral will be on Wednesday."

"Did you ask about the keys?" Neil fitted a handful of forks into the rack.

"Put those in with the tines down," Connor said. "Otherwise, whoever unloads them will get stabbed. Yes, William has one key, and Gerald said he has one on his key ring, and there should be another one on his wife's. Yesterday, he gave me the spare that hung on a rack in the kitchen. Also, a neighbor has one. She came in to water plants if they went away. That's all he could think of."

"Five keys," Neil said, reaching to flip the forks en masse. "Ouch."

"Told ya. We'd better round those keys up tomorrow. William and Gerald have theirs with them in Dover. Edna's should be in the house. Gerald thought it would be in her purse in the bedroom. We'll have to visit the neighbor and see if she's got hers. He gave me the name and address."

Adrienne came in, leading Matthew by the hand. "Hey, guys! We're going to go out and build a snowman. Want to help?"

They all bundled up and went into the front yard and began construction. Matthew and Connor took charge of making the biggest snowball, for the base. Neil came to help Kate, and soon they were working together, laughing, as they rolled a stomach for the snowman. Adrienne made a smaller ball for the head, then ran into the house to get a carrot and some big buttons for eyes. While she was gone, Connor and Matthew began a playful snowball fight.

"I don't think I'll get into that," Kate said, eyeing her brother-in-law warily.

Neil's eyes glittered as he stooped for a handful of snow and began shaping it. He packed it into a round, smooth ball.

"That had better not be for me," Kate warned.

Neil grinned and took aim at Connor as he chased his son across the yard. *Splat.*

Connor turned and gaped at him. "You didn't."

"Kate did it."

Kate opened her mouth in protest, then giggled when she saw the mischievous expression on Neil's face. She sobered as their eyes locked on each other.

"Are you seeing anyone?" Neil asked, looking down at her with shining brown eyes.

Splat! A soft snowball hit Neil's shoulder and exploded all over them, as Connor's laughter came from behind them.

An hour later, Connor walked with Neil to his truck.

"So," Connor said. "You and Kate are getting along well."

Neil eyed him thoughtfully.

"She seems willing to forgive and forget."

"Well, be careful."

Neil sighed. "I think we've had this conversation."

Connor raised one hand, as if in apology for saying it. "I'm only calling it like I see it. And I'd hate to see you and Kate pick up where you left off and self-destruct."

That hit him hard. "I'd like to think I'm past that."

"Yeah?" Connor's eyes narrowed. "Old habits are hard to break. You know you used to be wild."

"Not anymore."

"No, and you told me that you're staying away from relationships for now and concentrating on growing your faith. Don't let my sister-in-law distract you." He put his hand on Neil's shoulder. "Also, next week, when Harry Fowler retires, you'll be the senior detective in the Priority Unit. I'll be putting a lot of responsibility on you."

Neil looked across the street and inhaled the frosty air. Senior detective at age twenty-eight. He'd never expected that.

Connor was right. Kate could definitely be a distraction—from his faith and his work—that he just couldn't afford right now.

Connor punched him playfully. "Are you sure you don't want to stay for supper?"

"I promised my mother I'd be over there tonight. The second day of Christmas is almost as important as the first one for us."

Neil drove to his parents' and prepared to be fussed over. His sisters and their families were there again, and the meal was noisy. His grandmother, "Oma," pumped him for information about whether he had a "girl." He thought of Kate, then pushed the thought aside and shook his head no.

Just then, his mother called them all to the table. As his father carved the meat, she asked, "How's Captain Larson doing?"

"Fine, Mama." His mother adored Connor.

"Did his wife have that baby yet?"

"Not yet."

"The captain is a real gentleman," his father said, as Anneke held up her plate.

"Well, I'll tell you," Neil's mother said. "If I ever get arrested, I hope he's the one to take me in."

"Not me, Mama?"

Everyone laughed. Neil shook his head.

"So, what's up with this murder case you're so busy with?" Oma asked.

Neil outlined the investigation for them, giving only the bare bones. Oma loved to watch mystery movies, and she always wanted to hear about his latest police cases.

He ate a lot and turned down his father's offer of beer. Dennis and Marc, his two brothers-in-law, and his sister Anneke had some. Marianne was pregnant for the third time, so she wasn't drinking, but they all made no secret that they thought Neil was strange for not partaking anymore. He shrugged it off. He had tried to tell them that after he was saved he had no desire to drink anymore, but they refused to accept his explanations and kept offering him drinks every time he was home. He'd gotten to where he just said no, thanks.

He forced himself to keep his attention on the conversation, but his mind kept wandering to Kate Richards. She was probably doing something interesting that night. He wondered if she'd truly forgiven him. Could he do better in a relationship now? Could he relate to a woman in a way that would honor God?

"Come on, Neil, help me get the card table set up," his father called.

Great. Games until midnight. Neil liked to play cards, but he knew he'd put in a long day tomorrow. Yet there was no way he could leave his family's house early again.

"Sure, Papa." He jumped up to help his father.

At the police station the next morning, Connor and Neil brought the other detectives of their unit up to speed on the case. Connor assigned Harry Fowler, the senior detective who would retire at the end of the week, to processing the fingerprint evidence, and asked him to supervise Lance and Jimmy, the two newest members of the unit. They'd recently passed the detective's exam and were still new to the intense investigative work of the Priority Unit. Neil and fellow detective Tony Carlisle were tapped to return to the Rileys' house with Connor.

Tony had held detective's rank only a year. Neil was often paired with him and was expected to make sure Tony did everything by the book. That could be trying, as Tony was a bit of a hotshot and sometimes bordered on arrogant. His uncle was the current governor of Maine, which made some members of the police department resent him. Connor wouldn't tolerate favoritism in the Priority Unit. Tony received the same treatment as the other men, and Connor expected the same respect and precise work from him as he did from his other detectives.

When the three of them arrived at the brick house, Connor sent Tony and Neil to find the neighbor who had been entrusted with a house key while he went inside to look for Mrs. Riley's purse.

The neighbor, Mrs. Endicott, was older than the Rileys. She puttered around for a while and finally came up with the key, but she didn't want to give it to the men.

"How do I know you're really policemen?" she asked.

Tony was impatient, but Neil showed her his badge and ID a second time. He asked her if she'd like to call the station and confirm their identity. She did. The two men waited. Finally, she gave Neil the key.

"Thanks, Mrs. Endicott. Did you happen to notice anyone walking in the neighborhood, or any strange cars parked in the area Christmas morning?"

"No. Sorry. I wish I could help you. It's just terrible, what happened to Edna."

Neil and Tony left with the key.

"Talk about an old fussbudget," said Tony as they walked down the sidewalk toward the Rileys' house.

"Old people need to be careful," Neil replied. "She was right, we could have been anybody."

Connor had found Edna Riley's purse and the fifth key. "I just talked to Harry," he said when Neil and Tony entered the living room of the brick house. "All the fingerprints we got yesterday were Mr. or Mrs. Riley's."

"So the perp wore gloves," said Tony.

"Maybe. Tony, let's say you want to kill a woman, and she lets you in the front door. You shoot her. How do you leave?"

"By the front door."

"It was locked. All five keys are accounted for."

"So. I have an extra key you don't know about."

Connor nodded. "Any number of people could have made one. The Rileys kept the spare hanging in the kitchen, where anyone could 'borrow' it. The neighbor had one. Who knows how many people had access to that one? You're probably right. Somebody used one of these five or made a copy of his own."

They went back to the office, and Neil called the medical examiner's office. The autopsy wasn't finished, but the doctor had recovered the .22-caliber bullet.

"Carlisle, go get it," Connor said. "Run it on the IBIS system."

Neil doubted it would do any good, but anything was possible. If the bullet had been fired by a gun that had been entered in the Integrated Ballistics Identification System, they would find out.

"I'll be upstairs," Connor said. That meant the chief's office. Mike summoned Connor frequently, or came down one flight to confer with him in Priority.

Funny, during the three years Neil had been in the unit under Mike, he'd never been upstairs to the chief's office. But since July, when Mike Crowley became chief and Connor took over the unit, Neil had been up there maybe a dozen times. It used to be really scary. When a man was called to the chief's office, it was like being a schoolboy who was sent to the principal. Not anymore. When Connor went upstairs now, Neil figured either they were getting a new case to work on, or Connor and Mike were drinking coffee and catching up on the latest cases.

Mike actually joined them during their break most mornings and prayed with them, now that he was a Christian. The other guys in the unit knew that they'd better stay out of the break room between ten and ten-fifteen if they didn't want to go to a prayer meeting. Mostly, they stayed away. Jimmy Cook came once in a while.

When Connor came back from Mike's office, his face was grave. "Bring the men over here, Neil. We've got to pick up another case. There's been another murder."

FOUR

Kate was shocked to see a bouquet of roses on her desk when she walked into the newspaper office after lunch on Monday. Her pulse quickened as she hurried between the rows of workstations toward it.

"Hey, Kate, great job this weekend," one of the copy editors called.

"Thanks." She hurried to her desk and looked the flowers over. Very classy arrangement in a glass vase. She couldn't think of anyone who would send her flowers…unless Neil… No, he wouldn't. Would he? She found the card and opened it.

"Wow, roses," said one of the clerks. "Is it your birthday?"

"No. It's from Mr. Cleeves." The letdown feeling annoyed her. That was irrational. Her new boss, whom she'd slaved all weekend to impress, had sent her a flamboyant symbol of his approval. Why should she be disappointed?

"Kate, great story on the murder."

She looked up to find the senior reporter, Milton Henderson, standing by her desk. "Thank you."

"You must have put in a lot of hours over Christmas."

"I did, but it was worth it."

Henderson nodded and went back to his own desk when Kate's phone rang.

"Hello, Miss Richards. This is John Cleeves."

She gulped. "Hello. Thank you so much for the flowers, Mr. Cleeves."

"Well, you did an excellent job on your stories about the Riley murder."

"Thank you, sir."

"Could you please step into my office for a minute?"

She walked across the room swiftly, trying to control her wobbly knees.

"Sit down, Kate," Cleeves said, indicating a chair opposite his desk. "What do you have planned for this afternoon?"

"Uh…" She zipped mentally through her options. "I've started an update on the Riley murder. I interviewed several of the victim's friends this morning. I intend to contact Captain Larson's unit to see if they have a report from the medical examiner yet and find out how their investigation is going."

"Good. But we just heard on the scanner that there's another homicide in the city. Since you have such a good rapport with the detective squad now, I thought I'd have you do the initial write-up about it. I can put Milt Henderson on the Riley murder follow-up if that's too much for you."

She inhaled carefully. "I think I can handle it, sir."

"Okay. Well, Milt is interviewing the mayor at one-thirty, but don't hesitate to ask him for help later if you need it. I want you to know that I have complete confidence in you."

"Thank you, sir. That means a lot to me."

He nodded. "Get as much as you can on the new case, but leave yourself time to finish the Riley update. Oh, and I have you down for the Rotary auction tomorrow night. You'll still be covering that, so pace yourself."

Kate returned to her desk and stared down at the notes she had scrawled while Cleeves talked. She was amazed that he had handed her another major story. Was this some kind of a test? Until last weekend, she had produced one news story a day and several short local briefs. It seemed she had paid her dues and was now considered a full-fledged reporter; the schedule Cleeves had just handed her proved that. She'd be lucky to have time to do her laundry. The scent of the beautiful roses seemed to mock her. This is what you wanted, isn't it?

Her cell phone rang, and she dug it out of her purse. She didn't recognize the number.

"Hello, this is Kate."

"Hi, Kate. Connor gave me your number. I hope you don't mind."

Neil. She felt a prickle of anticipation at the sound of his deep voice. "I don't mind. Thanks for calling."

"Connor asked me to tell you that our public liaison will hold a press conference at four this afternoon."

"About the Riley case? I mean…I heard there was another murder."

"Wow. Word travels fast. They'll probably discuss both cases."

"I'll be there. The editor just told me I'm covering the new case, too."

"Great," Neil said. "Connor has put me in charge of the new case while he and some of the other detectives continue on the Riley murder. I'm headed for Deering now."

"Will you be at the press conference?" she asked.

"I'll probably be busy. But you can call me if you need anything. I can tell you that the medical examiner sent the bullet that killed Edna Riley over here for testing."

"Thanks. That will give me a start for my update story. Can I call you later to see what the tests show, or will that come out in the press conference?"

"It depends on what we find out. Why don't you give me a call?"

She hesitated. "I could come to the new crime scene."

"I don't know, Kate. Reporters kind of get in the way at a crime scene."

"I'll wait, like I did Saturday. I don't want to miss anything, Neil."

"Well…okay. I expect some other journalists have heard about it, too."

He gave her the address, and she hung up feeling more confident. With hard work, she could get the basics of the new murder case this afternoon, and she could finish the Riley update on her laptop while she waited for Neil to brief her. And Neil was now her contact at the police department. A few days ago, that would have disturbed her, but now she smiled as she headed for her car.

Neil wasn't used to supervising an entire team, but Connor assigned Tony Carlisle and Jimmy Cook to go to the new crime scene in the Deering neighborhood with him.

"You'll also have four uniformed officers and a crime scene tech at your command," Connor said.

"Okay." Neil opened his bottom desk drawer and pulled out a necktie. "Tell me again why we got this case, not the detective squad?" He looped the tie around his neck and flipped his collar down over it.

"The chief saw similarities to the Riley case, so he called me upstairs. I agree with him—it looks like the same M.O. A neighbor found your victim dead in his home, and the first responders indicated the cause of death looked like a gunshot wound."

"Got it." Neil patted his pockets to make sure he had all his equipment. "Tony, Jimmy, let's go."

The three men left the Priority Unit office and headed for the scene. The next hour passed in a whirl. The first responders had secured the scene, but it was up to Neil and his men to find and process any evidence. Fifteen minutes after he arrived, Neil went to his truck for extra gloves and saw Kate Richards's car parked at the curb beyond the lawn. She waved. He nodded and quickly went inside. Now he knew how Connor had felt on Saturday.

The run-down house wasn't exactly spotless, and the four cats' litter box needed changing. They hovered about the kitchen yowling while the men took blood samples and dusted the door frame for fingerprints. Neil turned to get his camera and stepped on a cat's paw. It screeched, and he jumped back, slamming into Jimmy. "Get them out of here!"

"Sure thing." Good-natured Jimmy grabbed one cat and shut it in a bedroom. The other three hopped about the kitchen, just out of his reach. One sprang from the counter to the top of the refrigerator and down onto a microwave oven topped with cereal boxes. The resulting avalanche took Neil's exasperation to a new level.

"Maybe they're hungry," Jimmy suggested.

"Brilliant." Neil was a bit chagrined he hadn't thought of the obvious. "Look for cat food." Tony found several cans in a cupboard and soon had the four cats wolfing a late dinner in the corner. Neil wiped his brow and wondered how much evidence the cats had compromised.

At quarter past two, he paused to sign off on evidence to be logged and remembered Kate. The medical examiner had left and a hearse rolled into the driveway. Neil took out his cell phone and called her.

"I'm sorry, Kate. I haven't had a minute to brief you. Why don't you just go do whatever else you need to do and call me in an hour?"

"Well…there's a TV crew setting up out here. I think I'll wait."

Neil sighed. "Okay. I'll try to come out soon and give you all something." As soon as he'd hung up, his phone rang.

"Hey, buddy, how are you doing?"

"Hey, Captain. It's real hectic here. I think we're doing everything right. Mostly. But there's so much going on, and the cats are driving me crazy."

"Cats?"

"Yeah. Four of them."

"Hmm. I wanted to let you know that Lance ran the bullet from the Riley case on the IBIS system, but didn't find any matches."

"That's too bad. I was hoping."

"Yeah," Connor said. "I went around to Riley's house and took down the crime scene tape. We got her medical records, and I've sent Harry to Riley's lawyer's office to get a copy of Mrs. Riley's will."

Neil took out his notebook and jotted down the pertinent facts. "Say, a bunch of reporters are out front, including Kate. Can I let them have this information?"

"Knock yourself out."

"Thanks. Oh, hold on, Connor, I think one of the victim's relatives just arrived." Neil squinted toward the door. One of the uniformed officers was leading a middle-aged woman toward the house. "Yeah, looks like it could be family. I'll call you later."

"Detective Alexander," the officer at the door said, "Mr. Hepburn's sister just arrived."

"Take her into the living room," Neil said. "I'll talk to her now." He braced himself and sent up a quick prayer. *Lord, You know I hate this part. But I can do it with Your help. Just help me not to say anything stupid.*

He pulled in a deep breath. This was part of the investigating officer's job. Neil wasn't sure he was ready for all that came with the position. The fact that Connor and the police chief had confidence in him carried a lot of weight. *Heavenly Father, let me live up to their expectations.*

He took off his latex gloves and went into the living room. The woman sat on the threadbare couch, staring at him. She wore blue knit slacks and a stained sweatshirt. Her graying hair looked as though she had raked her hands through it many times.

"Hello, ma'am. I'm Detective Alexander. I'm in charge of the case."

"An officer came to my house and told me my brother was dead."

"Yes, ma'am. I'm very sorry about Mr. Hepburn."

"What happened?"

"We're trying to find that out."

"It must not have been natural causes, or there wouldn't be so many policemen here, and Channel 2 wouldn't have sent a news crew."

Neil sighed. "You're right. Your brother was shot."

"Shot? By who?"

"We don't know, ma'am. The medical examiner will perform a full examination of your brother's remains."

"An autopsy?"

"Yes, ma'am." Neil expected her to protest.

She eyed him thoughtfully for a long moment. "I don't guess they'd let me watch."

Neil held back a startled cough. "Uh…no, I don't think so."

She nodded. "I'd probably get upset, anyway. But I enjoy those crime shows. Always thought I should have been a medical examiner or an FBI agent."

"What do you do, ma'am?"

"I'm retired, but I was a kindergarten teacher for forty years."

Neil allowed her a brief look at her brother's body before the men from the funeral home removed it. She identified the corpse and gave Neil some details about Theodore. She also offered to take the cats home with her, to Neil's great relief.

At last he got outside to give a brief press conference. Kate stood with the other reporters and didn't let on that she knew him personally. Neil was glad. He rattled off the data he could release and answered a good-natured question about the cats the reporters had seen the patrolmen remove from the house, then went back inside to continue working.

At the end of the day, he drove to the office to write up his reports. It was after five o'clock, and Connor wasn't at his desk. Neil hesitated, then called the Larson house. Adrienne answered.

"Hi, Neil. Are you coming over for supper?"

"Am I supposed to?"

"I told Connor to tell you."

"I haven't seen him since this morning," Neil said.

"Oh. Well, he called me at noon, and I told him to bring you home for supper. Kate's running late, too. I guess everyone's had a busy day."

On impulse, he stopped on the way for flowers for Adrienne.

His mother had taught him that a gift for the hostess was always appropriate. He felt like getting some for Kate, too, but restrained himself from the impulsive gesture, afraid it might be misunderstood.

Both sisters greeted him with huge smiles and exclaimed over the bouquet.

"I took Matthew and went shopping for Christmas cards and wrapping paper this morning," Adrienne said, when he commented that she looked a little tired.

"Kind of late, isn't it?" he asked.

"Oh, Neil, the best sales are the day after Christmas. Or at least, the next business day after Christmas. This stuff is for next year."

She showed him the things she had bought—cards, ribbon, gift wrap and bags, candles, ornaments and strings of lights. "When Connor comes home, I just have to get him to haul it all upstairs to the spare room."

"I'll do it."

"Would you? That would be terrific. Kate can show you where I want it."

She gave them instructions, and Kate and Neil managed to carry everything up and stow it in a closet.

Kate was beautiful, Neil decided anew—even in jeans and a Skowhegan Indians sweatshirt. Her cheeks were a little flushed, and her eyes glittered as she pushed bags up onto the shelf and stacked boxes on the closet floor. A package of bows fell off the shelf and hit her on the head. She laughed and stooped to pick it up. He laughed, too, took it from her and flung it hard up onto the back of the shelf.

"Guess we wouldn't make very good elves," she said.

"Nope. Elves have been tossed out of the North Pole for squishing bows. Get your stories done?"

"Yes. I would have liked a little more detail on the Riley case. Connor told me about Mrs. Riley's will."

"What about her will? I haven't had a chance to talk to Connor about that."

"Mrs. Riley had some money of her own. She left bequests to a couple of her favorite charities, and the rest will revert to her husband."

"How much?"

Kate shrugged. "Not much, as estates go. I believe she left ten thousand dollars to her garden club, another ten thousand to the animal shelter and about thirty thousand to her husband. It's in my notebook, but I'm pretty sure those were the figures."

"Hmm. Probably more than Theodore Hepburn's estate is worth. Hey, Kate?"

"Yeah?" She looked up at him with those big, deep blue eyes and something clutched in his stomach.

"I didn't mean to snub you today."

"No problem. We're both professionals. I knew you were busy."

They went down the stairs and discovered that Connor was home. His briefcase sat on the kitchen floor at his feet, and he was holding Matthew in one arm and kissing Adrienne passionately. Neil pulled Kate back into the living room and said, "Maybe we should just give Santa and Mrs. Claus a minute to say hello."

Kate laughed again, a wonderful sound that warmed him all the way through. What had he lost when he'd pushed their relationship too fast last summer? He plugged in the Christmas tree lights and went over to the CD player. "Want some music?"

"Sure. How about Christmas carols?"

They sorted through the CDs, and Kate picked one that was all instrumental carols and put it on.

"Did you get to the press conference at the police station?" Neil asked.

"Yes, but I already knew most of the information they released. I did get a couple of questions in, but I got more from what you told me than I did from the official spokesman."

"Glad I could help you. We should have more tomorrow, though. Today was kind of a plodding day. It takes time to slog through the evidence and interviews." He looked toward the doorway. "Think it's safe now?"

Kate peeked around the doorjamb and through the sunroom at the kitchen. "Can't see anybody."

"Maybe we should just make noise and go on in," Neil said.

They went to the kitchen door and he said loudly, "So, Connor, how'd it go on the Riley case?"

Connor was leaning against the counter in the corner where the telephone hung, holding Matthew and watching Adrienne make salad. Her hair was all loose and swung down her back, below her hips. Neil was sure it had been in a ponytail when he'd arrived.

"Not bad," Connor said. "We'll need to compare notes in the morning and see how many similarities the two cases have."

"Locked houses, for one thing," Neil said.

"Really? Not an open window upstairs?"

"No. Not that."

"Did you have the guys lift prints?" Connor asked.

"Yeah, all over the kitchen."

Connor looked at Kate. "So, how are you doing today, ace reporter?"

She smiled. "Not bad. I managed to write a stellar update on the Riley case and a brilliant piece on the Hepburn murder, thanks to Neil."

He returned her smile. It felt good not to be an outcast any longer.

They sat down to supper, and afterward played Rook at the kitchen table. Neil told them about the cats and had them all laughing over the detectives' wild feline chase. By nine o'clock, he felt he should leave, although he enjoyed sitting beside Kate and laughing over nothing. He hadn't had so much fun in ages. But Adrienne looked tired, and Connor was drooping a little, too. When the round ended, he said, "I'd better get going. I'll see you tomorrow, Connor."

"Good night, Neil."

Kate got up and walked toward the entry with Neil.

"So, will I see you again soon?" he asked.

Kate looked away, but she was smiling.

"What?" Neil asked.

"I have a feeling you're going to see a lot of me. I decided to move in here. Tomorrow after work I'm going to bring some of my stuff over. I think I can bring a little every day and be all moved by the end of the week. I told my roommates, and they didn't pout and beg me to stay."

"You're too mature for them."

She chuckled. "Yeah, and I didn't ask for a refund on the next month's rent I already gave them."

"Hey, I could help you with my truck."

"That's okay. But thanks."

"All right." Take it slow and easy, he reminded himself. "So, I guess I'll see you sometime."

"Maybe Wednesday," she said. "I really like Connor and Adrienne's church, and if they go to prayer meeting on Wednesday, I think I'll go with them. And I'll probably be hounding you for updates on the homicides."

"Right." Neil zipped his coat and said good-night with a smile.

Neil and Connor hashed over the two cases over steaming cups of black coffee early the next morning at the station.

"Mr. Hepburn was found lying in his kitchen by his neighbor, Mrs. Poulin," Neil said. "She tried to call him Saturday to tell him one of his cats was after the birds at her feeder, and got no answer. Yesterday, she tried again and still no answer, so she went over. No one came to the door, and she looked in a window and saw him lying there and called it in. Small-caliber gunshot to the heart. No weapon found in the house. All doors and windows locked."

"Robbery?" Connor asked.

"Don't think so. His wallet was on his dresser. He lived alone, but his sister lives in town, and his children have been notified. The oldest daughter should arrive today."

"Where are you heading with it now?"

"The usual," Neil said. "We'll run the ballistics and the fingerprints, question the neighbors, look for a motive. Do you think these two cases are related?"

"That question came up at yesterday's press conference. They look alike in several ways, but it's too soon to be sure."

Chief Mike Crowley came in through the door that led to the stairway and walked over to Connor's desk.

"You guys ready for an early prayer meeting? I've got to spend a couple of hours with the new deputy chief this morning, and I didn't want to go into it without prayer."

The new deputy had started his job in Portland the day before. Mike had been without a deputy for several months and was hoping the new man, Jack Plourde, could take some of the pressure off him. Plourde's résumé looked good, but he was still an unknown quantity.

They went into the break room, and the three of them prayed about Plourde and the homicide cases, and for Adrienne's health and the baby's. Neil prayed for wisdom in trying to talk to his family about his savior.

When Mike left them, Connor said to Neil, "Adrienne and I are supposed to have our last Lamaze class tonight, but she's not feeling great."

"Uh, that would be natural childbirth lessons?" Not exactly a topic Neil was well versed in.

"Right. To help Adrienne when she delivers the baby."

"And you're doing this voluntarily?"

Connor smiled. "Of course. I want to be there when it happens. The classes teach the father what to do to help the mother."

"What, like getting the doctor to put her to sleep?"

Connor laughed. "I don't expect you to understand this yet, Neil. The whole pregnancy thing is an adventure. I want to be part of every phase, including the birth. The baby is God's gift to us."

"I know, Connor, but isn't it kind of…"

"What?"

"Oh, I dunno." What did it seem like? Embarrassing? Alarming? Frightening?

"No, it's not. Whatever you're thinking, it's not. It's fantastic."

"If you say so. Did you take these classes before Matthew was born?"

"No, but Adri and I both wish we had."

Neil nodded. "I just can't see what's so appealing about a roomful of pregnant women sitting around telling you how rotten they feel."

"I'll remind you someday that you said that." Connor sighed. "I feel like I'm at a dead end on the Riley case. We've pretty much ruled out Gerald Riley, and I don't have any other suspects."

"I know what you mean. But you always tell me to keep on following the evidence. Something will break."

The elevator moaned and the doors opened. Kate Richards stepped off, looking sophisticated in a gray skirt suit and high heels. Neil leaped to his feet, finding it slightly hard to breathe. He'd thought he was beyond being dazzled by a woman. Apparently not.

Connor stood, too. "Hello, Kate. You found us all right."

"No problem." She smiled at Neil. "Hi."

Connor said, "The city editor called this morning and asked if I'd give Kate a few minutes for an exclusive interview."

"Wow. That's great."

"Kate's editor was so impressed with the stories she did over the weekend that he wants an in-depth piece about our unit."

"I hope I'm not interrupting your investigation," Kate said.

"No," Neil said. "We were just talking about the Riley case."

"That's right." Connor looked toward the windows. A few snowflakes fluttered down outside, but it didn't look serious. "We don't think Mr. Riley killed his wife, largely for two reasons. We didn't find any gunshot residue on him, and we haven't found the weapon."

Kate nodded. "I hear you. If he did it, how did he get rid of the gun?"

"And if he did do it, we should have found residue on his hands and his clothes," Connor added.

"Even if he washed his hands and changed his clothes?" Kate asked.

"Yeah," Neil said. "Most people don't get it off when they wash up, and we checked all his laundry for that very reason."

Connor lifted his hands in resignation. "It had to be an outsider."

"But why would an outsider do that?" Neil asked. "Why would he go into someone's house on Christmas Day, shoot an old lady, not steal anything, go out and lock the door, leaving her lying on the floor by a loaded Christmas tree?"

"Were the Christmas presents opened?" Kate said.

"What?" Neil asked.

"The Rileys' Christmas packages. The gun could be in one of them. Did you open them when you searched the house?"

FIVE

"Oh, come on. That's too…" Neil stopped. He and Connor looked at each other. "You know the gun went out the door with the shooter, Connor."

"*If* he went out the door. If he stayed, maybe the gun stayed."

"So what do you want me to do?"

"Go open the gifts."

"Oh, come on. We both know Gerald Riley didn't do it."

"I'll keep wondering about him if you don't do this. Take another officer with you. I'll call Brad. Take some tape and seal them up again after. And be very careful with the paper. I've got to go do this interview with Kate. Do it now, Neil." Connor picked up his phone and called downstairs, asking the day patrol sergeant for a uniformed officer to work on the detail.

Neil knew sputtering would do no good, so he put on his jacket.

"Kate, let's go into our interview room," Connor said. "I'll get us some coffee, and we—" His phone rang, and he picked it up with a grimace. "Sorry."

Kate smiled and shrugged.

"What?" Connor asked, an urgency creeping into his voice. "Okay. Yeah. Are you all right? I'll be there in…" He glanced at his watch. "Twenty minutes. Got it." He hung up. "I'm sorry, Kate, but it looks like we'll have to reschedule. Adri's water broke. I'm meeting her at the hospital."

Kate's jaw dropped. "She's not supposed to go for another three weeks."

"I know. Tell that to the baby." Connor grabbed his coat.

Kate chased him to the stairway door. "What about Matthew? Should I go home?"

"No, Adri said the pastor's wife is picking him up and driving her to the hospital. I'll call you later."

"Should I come with you?"

"Well, it could take hours. I'll see you there later."

The door shut behind him. Kate turned and looked at Neil. "Now what?"

Neil wiggled his eyebrows at her. "I don't suppose you feel like unwrapping gifts?"

She laughed. "Might as well, if you're sure I'm allowed."

"Well, it's not officially a crime scene anymore. If the Riley family is at the house, I'll just ask their permission to look around again."

The house was still empty, and Neil felt a little bit like a trespasser as they entered. He opened the first gift with trepidation. A cordless drill. He tried to put the paper back on exactly the way it had been, but he couldn't make the edges fold right.

"Hey, why don't you let me do that?" Kate asked. "You open them, I'll wrap them up again."

"Great idea."

An hour later, all of the gifts had been opened, checked and rewrapped for nothing.

"Sorry." Kate stared mournfully at the heap of packages. "It seemed like a good idea at the time."

"That's okay," Neil said. "At least we've been thorough. Let's get some lunch."

They stopped at a fast food place for burgers. Kate left him to return to the newspaper office afterward, and Neil went back to the station.

Tony Carlisle was running the ballistics on the Hepburn case. "Neil, can you come look at this?" There was an edge to Tony's voice.

Neil went over and stood behind him. "Did you match it to a gun?"

"No, but it brought up the images from the bullet you ran yesterday. Look." He toggled between them. "Riley. Hepburn. Riley. Hepburn."

"Yikes." They had the same configuration. The same groove on one side. There wasn't any doubt. It was a definite match.

Neil called Connor's cell phone.

"The bullets match but we still don't have a weapon," he told Connor.

"No, but we'll get one. Tell Tony I said good work. At least now we know these two murders were committed with the same gun."

"Right," Neil said. "How's Adri doing?"

"Okay. Slow progress."

Neil didn't think he wanted any more details. He hung up and checked on what the other detectives had learned.

"Do you have a time of death on Hepburn?" he asked Jimmy Cook.

"Between five and nine p.m. Sunday night."

"And Mrs. Riley died between eight and nine a.m. Saturday." Neil sat down in his chair and leaned back, thinking about that.

"Tony mentioned there might be a witness," Jimmy said.

Tony shook his head. "Some girl saw a guy walk down the street Sunday evening. Nothing, really. She couldn't describe him, and there was no reason to think it was peculiar. It was about five-thirty, and I suppose it could be significant."

Neil nodded. "Harry and Lance are still canvassing the neighborhood, trying to find someone else who saw him."

"Was this Hepburn rich?" Jimmy asked.

"No. Definitely middle-class. His house was appraised at a hundred and thirty thousand, but I think most of that was for the location. It's not in very good shape. His furniture was run-down, utilitarian stuff. I saw his checkbook. Three-hundred-dollar balance, checks this month for phone and lights, insurance, one credit card. Not a big spender, for sure."

"The Rileys were pretty well off," Tony said.

Jimmy threw Neil a sympathetic look. "Too bad you had to unwrap all the packages."

Tony chuckled. "Yeah, Kate Richards is pretty, but I don't think she's so brilliant. Come on, a killer wrapping up a gun in a Christmas present?"

Neil shrugged. "It's okay. We should have checked them anyway. And we know for sure now the gun didn't stay in Riley's house." He had a sudden thought that made him want to scream. "Oh, no."

"What?" Jimmy asked.

"What if the shooter stole one of the packages?"

Tony and Jimmy stared at him for a moment.

"No," Tony said. "Kate sent you off on one wild-goose chase. We're not going down another road to nowhere."

"Thank you," Neil said.

"You're welcome."

"I suppose we could ask Mr. Riley if any are missing, just in case."

Neil reviewed Mrs. Riley's medical records and obituary. He opened his notebook and went over the information they'd taken from the family.

Everyone loved Edna Riley. She attended garden club and volunteered for medical causes and fund-raisers for the Animal Protection Society. She collected money for breast cancer research and walked dogs for the shelter. She'd worked for a few years as a typist in the dean's office at the college where her husband had taught, but hadn't worked outside the home in years. Neil felt he was spinning his wheels. She was just a sweet old grandma, and Mr. Hepburn was an old man who liked cats. So who would kill them?

At eight that evening, Neil laid down his latest *Police* magazine to answer his ringing cell phone.

"Hey, Neil, it's Connor. It's a girl."

"Congratulations!" Neil grinned. "What's her name?"

"Hailey. Or Chloe. We can't decide."

"Well, you've had nine months." Neil chuckled. If it were up to Connor, the decision would probably have been made long ago. "How is everybody?"

"Adri's fine. The baby's a little jaundiced. They may keep her an extra day. I think I'll take tomorrow off and bring Matt in to see his mom. If the baby's doing better, she can come home, but if not, we'll just leave her and Adri both here in the hospital another night."

Neil gulped. "Okay. What should I be doing?"

"The same thing you do every day. Just ride herd on the boys and make sure they do their paperwork. Especially Carlisle. He's got a great mind, but he leans toward lazy sometimes."

"Yeah. Uh…is there anything I can do for you and Adri?"

"I don't think so," Connor said. "Kate picked Matthew up from the pastor's house, and she's staying with him tonight. I'll stay here with Adri tonight. I might take the rest of the week off."

Neil's stomach dropped. Taking over a case was one thing, and being in charge while Connor took an afternoon off hadn't been so bad. But three more days? He reminded himself that when Connor took vacation this year, he'd have to stand in for the captain. As of Monday, Neil would be the senior detective. Might as well start acting like it.

"Hey, I think you should." *Did I just say that?*

"Really?"

"Sure." Neil cleared his throat. "We've got everything under control."

"Did you check those packages?"

"Yeah, nothing suspicious in them. You go ahead and take some time off. You need time with Adri, and when the baby comes home, you'll be short on sleep anyway."

"You sure?"

"Absolutely." Neil gritted his teeth. *Lord, help me not to regret this.*

* * *

Kate sat at her desk Friday, staring with unfocused eyes at her notebook. No matter how many times she went over her notes, nothing new popped out at her. But the city editor wanted another major story on the Riley case by five o'clock.

On Wednesday, Neil had given her the news that the ballistics tests matched the bullets in the Riley and Hepburn cases. Kate had written up the story and a sidebar in which she explained the IBIS system, courtesy of Neil's buddy Tony Carlisle. Tony had seemed delighted to give her a demonstration and answer her questions. He'd also asked her for a date, which Kate had declined. Tony seemed like the kind who didn't take anything seriously outside his job. Not her type, though she'd enjoyed the hour she spent interviewing him.

Thursday she'd gotten by with a brief update. *Nothing new in the Riley and Hepburn murder cases, according to Detective Neil Alexander, chief investigator….* She couldn't get away with that again today, even though she'd turned in two other stories unrelated to the murders. She felt her stock was falling rapidly at the *Press Herald*.

In desperation, she decided to call the president of Edna Riley's garden club. Maybe some of the club members would share poignant memories of Edna. If that didn't work, she could try the animal shelter, where Edna had volunteered.

Kate sighed. It was fluff, and she knew it. Maybe she could call Ted Hepburn's sister, although she shrank from doing that. Fishing for leads from a woman whose brother had just been murdered seemed a little crass. She wanted a good, meaty article that would give the readers something new and solid. She'd also been assigned to copy the police blotter for the next day's paper. Ordinarily, she would have put that off until her other stories were finished, but on impulse, she decided to drive to the police station right away and get that chore done. Maybe she could touch base with Neil or Tony in person, get some brilliant new information on the murder cases and watch her stock rise again.

* * *

Neil had worked on the homicides all week, but seemed no closer to solving them. It was Harry Fowler's last day, and everyone seemed to think they should knock off early for his retirement party.

"Detective Alexander, Miss Richards is on line one."

The secretary's alert left him a bit annoyed and yet slightly hopeful—annoyed because Kate called frequently, wanting updates on the cases when he wasn't prepared, and hopeful because she seemed willing to overlook his past indiscretions. A part of him hoped she was calling because she wanted to talk to him.

Okay, he'd admit it—he missed her. Beyond the intense physical attraction he'd felt when he first met her, he'd seen a sweet determination he admired. He'd made the mistake of treating her like he had a hundred other girls, and expecting her to respond as they would. But Kate was a Christian. She'd enjoyed being with him, that was obvious. She'd seen him nearly every night for two weeks, against her sister's warnings. But when he'd pushed her to take the relationship beyond her comfort zone, Kate's faith had kicked in. At the time, he'd laughed and said she was too inhibited. She'd pleaded with him to take it slowly. Why hadn't he listened? Instead he'd said some cruel things. The blowup that followed shocked him. Not only had Kate walked away in tears and returned to Skowhegan the next day, but Connor had come after him and warned him strongly to keep away from his sister-in-law—this coming from his captain and friend. The pain he'd caused others had brought Neil up short and forced him to reconsider his own lifestyle.

Connor had witnessed to him dozens of times before, but Neil had laughed it off and told him, "Maybe later, when I've had my kicks." But the month of July was a watershed, when he'd seen himself from God's perspective.

He wanted to do things God's way now that he was saved, but his confidence in the romance department had plummeted. He'd done everything wrong before. How could he learn to do it right?

He took a deep breath and picked up his phone. "Hi, Kate. How you doing?"

"Hey, Neil. I'm fine. I'm downstairs at the patrol sergeant's desk, actually."

"Oh?" Neil put his hand to his forehead. How could he get out of inviting her up to the office for a chat? He didn't need a reporter chat right now, and looking into those huge blue eyes would probably just distract him for the rest of the day.

"I've just been going over the police log for the paper, and I saw something kind of weird. Did you hear about the cat shooting yesterday?"

Neil sat up straight and lowered his hand. "No. What's that about?"

"It seems the dispatcher took a call from a woman who said someone shot at her cat. Two patrol officers responded, and sure enough, there was the woman with her cat. It had a graze on its hind leg. They got a statement from the owner and picked up some empty .22 cases. She gave them a description of the kid who did it and showed them the exact spot of the 'attempted murder' as she called it."

"Oh, yeah?" Neil scratched his head. It was odd, but he wouldn't have thought it newsworthy.

"Yeah. As it happened, one of the responding officers was here when I read it. He told me there was a little blood on the snow, so he dug around and pried a bullet out of the dirt."

"The bullet that hit the cat?"

"Maybe. He said it wasn't something they would usually follow up on, but…"

Neil frowned, wondering exactly what Kate wanted of him. "We don't have time to run something like that on the IBIS system. We've got more serious crimes to investigate." *Like the two murders I'm stuck on.*

"I suppose you're right. I was just thinking that maybe that bullet could be from a gun that was used in another crime. When Tony showed me how the system works the other day, I was very impressed. I guess I got a little carried away with my enthusiasm. Sorry. I shouldn't have bothered you."

"Whoa, wait." Neil knew it was ridiculous, but for some reason, he felt like a heel. He could almost see Kate's blue eyes, filled with contrition. "Who's the officer? I'll talk to him. Maybe I could find time to just give it a quick run on my lunch hour. And thanks, Kate."

"Nuts," he said when he hung up a minute later. "I am absolutely nuts."

"What's up?" Tony asked from across the aisle.

"Nothing to do with our cases. Just a favor for someone." Neil asked himself what Connor would do in this situation, and he knew the answer. Forget it! But he'd committed himself to at least ask Patrolman Ray Oliver about it now. Reluctantly, he called the patrol sergeant and asked if Oliver was in. Five minutes later, the patrolman called him on his desk phone.

"Oh, that girl reporter got to you?" Oliver asked, when Neil inquired about the shooting. "She's pretty, but this is a low-priority incident."

"Where's the bullet now?" Neil asked, deliberately avoiding his question.

"In the evidence room. If you guys want to log it out and play with it, well…knock yourself out. I don't have time to mess with stuff like that."

Ten minutes later, Neil had the bullet in the lab and began the test. "I must be bonkers."

The screen flashed, and Neil stared at it. He grabbed his phone and dialed Connor's cell phone.

"What's up, Neil?" the captain asked.

"This is crazy, but Kate gave me a tip about a kid shooting at a cat this morning. A patrolman recovered a bullet. Connor, it matches the bullets from the two murders."

Connor whistled softly. "Look, I'm on the way home with Adrienne and the baby. I'll come to the police station as soon as I get her settled."

"You don't need to."

"Well, I—" After a short pause, Connor said slowly, "You're right. I don't. You can handle this, Neil. You know what to do, don't you?"

"Yeah." It felt good, realizing that he knew exactly how to proceed. "We'll be fine, Connor."

"Great, because I shouldn't really leave Adri alone today with the baby and Matt. So just…go ahead with the investigation and bring me a full report. I'll be back at my desk Monday."

"Oh, uh…there's one thing. Since Kate gave me this tip, is it okay if I…?"

"I guess she earned it."

Neil smiled. "Thanks." He took out his cell phone and suddenly realized it contained a lot of baggage he no longer needed. Sarah Maguire. That was a mistake. Delete. Cyndi Plaisted. She got married, didn't she? Delete. Carol Zeigler. He couldn't remember who she was, or what she looked like. Delete.

When the directory was stripped down to numbers he actually used these days, he felt efficient and lonely. The exercise was a depressing reminder of his old lifestyle. Bringing up the newest number he'd added and remembering his purpose lifted the melancholia a little. When Kate answered with an inviting lilt in her voice, he felt even better.

"Kate, you're the best."

"What? Neil, is that you?"

"Yes, and I owe you big-time."

"You do?"

"I sure do. Remember your cat bullet? It matches the bullets from the Riley and Hepburn murders."

"Oh, wow! What now?"

"We'll be working in the neighborhood where the cat was shot. We need to find the young man who fired that gun."

"I'll go over there," Kate said quickly.

"Good. I think you can help us. Maybe I'll call a press conference, even. The media can help us locate that kid."

Twenty minutes later, the entire Priority Unit and a dozen patrolmen hit the neighborhood where the cat was shot, miles away from the two homicides.

Neil interviewed the cat owner personally. Mrs. Sargent had seen the boy clearly—she called him a boy—but she didn't know him. A female officer drove her to the police station, where Sergeant Lyons set her up with a sketch artist. By two o'clock, the officers had sketches and were showing them to everyone in the area. Neil called a press conference and released the sketch.

"The cat is going to be fine," he told the reporters who gathered in the lobby. "It has a minor wound, but a veterinarian has treated it, and he says it will heal. But the gun that wounded the cat has been linked to some other crimes, and the police department wants that gun and would like to talk to the person who used it." For the next ten minutes, he fielded questions from the television and newspaper reporters. He caught Kate's eye once, and she smiled at him. When it was over and the rest were rushing out the door, she made a beeline for where he stood.

"This is great, Neil!" Her blue eyes sparkled. "I told my editor, and I'm writing the story."

"Congratulations."

"So, you hope to find the person who shot the cat."

"I think we have a good chance. Several people have called in, but so far we haven't found the right guy. The sketch seems to look vaguely like a lot of people."

She nodded. "Maybe after they show it on the TV news tonight." She looked at her watch. "I'd better get at my story. Thanks again." She reached out to squeeze his arm, and her touch electrified him. Kate seemed to feel it, too, looking a little dazed as she gave him a quick smile and turned to go.

Neil waded through a mountain of reports brought in by the detectives following up on tips from people who thought they recognized the sketch of the cat shooter. They had nothing solid by the end of the day. Maybe, as Kate had said, someone who saw the evening news could make a positive identification.

He was just about to leave the office that evening when the dispatcher called him.

"Detective Alexander, we have a woman on the line with something that may interest you."

Neil waited while the dispatcher connected him. "Hello. How may I help you?"

"I wondered if the police department could send someone over here to pick up a gun."

"A gun, ma'am?"

"Yes."

"Is it your gun?"

"No, of course not." She sounded peeved. "I took my trash out a little while ago, and I saw a gun in my apartment building's Dumpster." She gave him an address three blocks from where the cat was shot.

Neil assured her an officer would be right over. "Bonus points for Kate Richards," he said as he hung up. Forty-five minutes later he'd recovered the pistol from the Dumpster and was back in the lab with it.

He took the serial number and dusted the pistol for prints. It had been wiped. Then he took it to the area where guns could be fired for ballistics testing in the lab.

Neil fired two rounds and put the bullets in the imaging camera. In a matter of minutes, he had the images running on the computer program for the ballistics matching system. The bullets he had test-fired matched the ones taken from the two homicide victims and the scene of the cat shooting.

Next, Neil traced the gun's serial number through computerized records. It was registered to a civilian, but had been reported stolen five years ago. He checked one more time to see if bullets from any other crimes matched that weapon, but got no more hits.

He sat back, satisfied. It was a moment to share. He decided to drive over to Connor's house and tell him what he had found. He arrived at the house at seven forty-five, and Kate met him at the door.

"Well, hi." She looked great, in an emerald-green sweater and jeans. The air between them seemed charged with electricity.

Neil smiled. "Hi. Is the boss home?"

"Yeah. He's in the bedroom with Adrienne and Hailey."

"Oh. I guess I should have called. I don't want to disturb him."

"It must be important, or you wouldn't have come over."

Neil couldn't hold back a grin. "It is."

"Anything I can know about?"

He hesitated. "Well…"

She shook her head. "I shouldn't have asked. Sorry. That's no way to repay you after what you did today. I mean, I called you with a flaky, long-shot idea, and you pursued it, and it paid off."

"I was really glad you told me about it. I don't usually pay much attention to stuff the patrolmen are dealing with."

"Come on in. Connor will probably want to hear whatever it is you've got. If I send you away, he and Adrienne will both say I shouldn't have."

Neil went inside with her. Matthew came padding in from the sunroom in his sleeper. "Uncle Neil!"

"Hey, buddy!" Neil swung him up in his arms. "So, you got a new sister, huh?"

Matt nodded solemnly.

Kate smiled at them. "Why don't you two go into the living room?"

Neil sat down on the couch with Matthew and picked up a picture book from the coffee table.

The captain entered a moment later. "Neil, what's up?"

Neil realized Kate was hovering in the doorway behind him. "I've got something good. I, uh, wasn't sure if I should tell Kate, though."

"Is it something you'll tell the world tomorrow?"

"Probably. And she did give us a major tip this morning. Should we let her break this in the morning paper?"

"Oh, please!" Kate rocked up and down on her toes with eagerness.

Connor gave her a tolerant smile. "You haven't had enough work for one day?"

"What is it?" She looked eagerly at Neil.

Absolutely gorgeous! Neil looked away from her vivid eyes. "Oh, just a little something I found tonight. Like the murder weapon in two homicides and an attempted cat-ricide."

Kate's jaw dropped. "You found the gun?"

"Found it and matched it to all three crimes."

"Good work," Connor said.

"This is huge! I've got to call my editor," Kate said.

"Do me a favor," Connor said. "You can say we found the murder weapon. Please don't reveal that it's the same gun used in the cat shooting."

Kate frowned. "All right." She turned and hurried to the kitchen.

"She'll be up half the night," Connor said. "And she'll probably want to ask you a million questions."

"It's okay," Neil said.

Matthew tugged on his sleeve. "Uncle Neil, the story."

They were halfway through the picture book when Kate returned with a preoccupied look. "Connor, my editor wants me to come in to the office and write the story there. Is that okay? Could you put Matt to bed?"

"Sure, but I hate for you to drive home late alone."

"I could take her," Neil offered. He was feeling good about his triumph, and he wondered if he was ready to spend a little more time with Kate.

"Are you sure?" she asked. "Because I really do need more details, and it would be great if you wanted to drive and I could take notes on the way."

"Perfect. My truck's in the driveway. Grab your notebook."

When they walked into the newsroom, the night editor rose from her chair.

"Hello, Kate. I hope you didn't mind coming in. I've got to remake the page, and I figured it would be easier if you put the story right into our system." The woman eyed Neil from behind her wire-framed glasses, then looked back at Kate.

"Jan, this is Detective Neil Alexander. He's the one who told me about the new evidence."

"Hello. Nice to meet you," the editor said. "Kate, your story will go on the split page."

"Not the front page?" Kate couldn't help hearing the disappointment in her own voice.

"We've got a scandal at the animal shelter already. Barry Patterson is working late on that story. We're getting close to deadline…." Jan glanced at the clock. "All right. Can you give me twelve inches in twenty minutes? I'll see what space I can free up on page one."

Kate gulped. She typed fast, but she wasn't sure she could translate her notes into readable copy that quickly.

"I'll do my best." She turned and looked at Neil. "You heard her. Want some coffee?"

"No, I'm good. What else do you need to know?"

It was the most intense interview Kate had ever done, but she pounded out the story in just under half an hour. She played up the discovery of the weapon, and that it positively connected the two murders. She sent the finished product electronically to Jan's computer.

"Not bad," Jan said when she opened the file. "I'm impressed, Kate. Barry is still on the phone with his source for that Animal Protection Society thing. Sounds like someone connected with the animal shelter made off with a pile of money."

Kate smiled and looked over at Neil. He winked at her, and her stomach fluttered. He was adorable, and instead of distracting her from her story, he'd helped her with it. A memory of kissing Neil in the summer sunlight flashed through her mind, but she quickly squelched it. "Thanks for letting me—" She whipped around to stare at Jan. "What did—" She turned back to Neil. "Did you hear what she said?"

"Yeah." Neil shook his head. "Too bad. Someone stole the shelter's money."

"They were going to build a new shelter, and one of the directors stole over a million dollars from their bank account," Jan said.

Neil whistled. "I wonder who's handling it at the police department."

"Barry could tell you, if he weren't on the phone," Jan said.

"Neil!" Kate grabbed his sleeve, certain there was more to the story. "Isn't that where Edna Riley volunteered?"

He looked down at her without speaking for a long moment. Finally, he inhaled. "She left them some money, too. Oh, man."

SIX

Neil watched as Connor skimmed the front page of Saturday morning's paper. Adrienne held the new baby on her lap as she ate breakfast. Kate circled the Larsons' kitchen table, pouring coffee for herself and the two men, and Matthew sat in his booster seat, eating oatmeal, between his parents' chairs.

"So," Connor said, "they've been planning this new four-million-dollar shelter for some time."

"Yeah." Neil reached for the sugar bowl. "The organization has been raising money for about two years. They had over half of what they needed and expected to break ground in the spring."

Connor nodded, still reading. "And yesterday the building fund was raided by the shelter's director, and he has apparently left town, according to Sergeant Legere's detectives."

"He might have left the state, or even the country," Neil said, "with over a million dollars."

"Pretty crummy." Kate slipped into her chair beside him.

Neil shot her a glance. "Kate's the one who made the connection. He could be our shooter."

Connor folded the papers and started reading a story below the fold. "So, Kate, I see you made page one again. Congratulations."

"Thanks." The toaster popped, and she jumped up to grab the toasted bagels.

"Don't you think we should do something to find this Burton guy who stole the money?" Neil asked.

Connor looked back at the top of the newspaper. "Jim Burton.

Well, Neil, I'll tell you. Two of Ron Legere's detectives are handling it. But that embezzler's not in Portland anymore, you can bet on that."

Neil's frustration made his coffee taste bitter, and he put an extra spoonful of sugar in it. "I spoke to Joey Bolduc last night. He's on the animal shelter investigation. When I called him, they were trying to find out if Burton had caught a plane. And the sergeant assured me his unit is doing everything possible to stop Burton if he hasn't left town yet, but they're afraid he's already skipped."

"So you really think this has to do with Mrs. Riley's murder?" Kate asked timidly.

"Not necessarily. Coincidences happen." Connor laid the paper beside his plate. "However, when one organization is involved in two major crimes in the same week, I take notice."

Neil thought back over all the information he had collected on Edna Riley. "Mrs. Riley left ten thousand dollars to the animal shelter, and she volunteered there, helping with the animals."

"Let's let the sergeant and his men see what they turn up this weekend," Connor said. "We may want to interview Professor Riley again on Monday."

"What about Hepburn, the second victim?" Kate asked. "I don't suppose he made a large bequest to the Animal Protection Society?"

"No, he didn't have much," Neil said. "His house was mortgaged. What little he had goes to his children."

Connor looked over the top of his newspaper. "Did his sister take the cats?"

Neil met his eyes. The facts slowly clicked into place in his mind. The two murder victims were both animal lovers. Kate watched him curiously.

Adrienne picked up on Connor's mood. "Sweetheart, you aren't going to work today, are you?"

"I wonder if Edna Riley knew Ted Hepburn," Connor said.

"Yeah. We could ask Mr. Riley," Neil suggested.

"Or we could call the shelter. What time do they open in the morning?"

"It's Saturday. I'm not sure they're open at all today."

"Somebody has to feed the animals," Connor said.

Adrienne let out a quiet moan.

Neil jumped up. "I'll go."

Connor nodded and reached over to give Adrienne's hand a squeeze. "Don't worry, honey. I told you I'll stay home this weekend. Neil's doing great on this case so far. I'm sure he can handle it."

Kate stood up, with half a bagel still in her hand. "I'll get my notebook, Neil. You're taking me, too, Neil. Please?"

One car sat in the parking lot of the animal shelter when Neil pulled in. He and Kate got out of the truck. Neil tried the handle on the shelter's front door, but it was locked. He knocked loudly. A red-haired woman in slacks and a ski sweater opened the door.

"May I help you?"

"I'm Detective Alexander with the Portland P.D., and I'm investigating the death of Mrs. Edna Riley."

"Terrible thing," she said.

"Yes, ma'am. May I ask you a few questions about Mrs. Riley?" He gestured at Kate. "This is Kate Richards of the *Press Herald.*"

The woman opened the door wide, and they followed her into the office area. It smelled like animals and shavings and dog food and manure. Somewhere beyond the office, dogs were barking.

The woman faced them. "I'm Roberta Palmer." She was forty or more, of medium build and pleasant. Not a model, by any means, but attractive. "How can I help you?"

"Mrs. Riley left the shelter a bequest," Neil said.

"Yes, ten thousand dollars. Her attorney informed us."

Neil asked, "Did the society receive that money yet?"

"No, thank heavens. If we had, it would have gone to Argentina, or wherever Jim Burton is now."

"I was very sorry to read about that, ma'am," Neil said.

"These poor animals are the ones who will suffer. We're so crowded here, and the facility is obsolete."

"So, will you have to cancel the new building?"

"I don't know. He didn't actually take *all* the money. There were some investments that he couldn't liquidate on his own. But he took the best part of it. Had it transferred electronically to some foreign bank, apparently. If he's not caught, I guess we have to start over. And people won't be so quick to donate a second time."

"No, ma'am."

"We're having a big fund-raiser next week," she said. "It's our annual fancy dinner dance, the Fur Ball. We expected to raise a huge amount of money, maybe as much as two hundred thousand dollars. But now I don't know if people will support it."

"And you and the other employees had no inkling—"

"Of course not!" She sounded offended.

"Did you know Edna Riley personally?" Neil asked.

"Oh, sure. Edna volunteered two days a week to brush the animals and take dogs out for a walk, or whatever we needed her to do. She was very helpful, and a good worker."

"How long had she done this?"

"Ten years maybe. She was devoted to the animals."

"But she didn't have any pets," Neil observed.

"Her husband was allergic." Roberta nodded sagely. "When she left here, she would go home and shower and wash her clothing so the dander wouldn't bother him."

Neil was aware of Kate standing behind him, listening avidly. She knew when to keep quiet. His conviction that she would succeed at her job ratcheted up a notch.

"Miss Palmer, did you know a man named Theodore Hepburn?" he asked.

"Ted Hepburn? Sure. He was another of our volunteers."

Neil glanced at Kate, who was writing quickly in her notebook. "He came in here regularly to help you out?"

"Yes. Every Friday," Roberta said. "He loved cats especially. He adopted several himself, ones we couldn't find a home for."

Riley stared at him in disbelief. His voice croaked a little when he said, "Ted? That was Ted from the shelter? I didn't connect it."

"Yes, sir. Did you know him?"

"Never met him, but on Fridays, Edna always came home with stories about Ted. He would flea-dip the dogs and things like that." He rubbed his jaw thoughtfully. "Yes. She did say… last Friday…Christmas Eve, that is…"

"Yes, sir? What did she say?"

Riley looked him in the eye. "Ted was upset that day. His daughter wanted him to go to her house over Christmas, and he didn't want to go. But there was something else. He told Edna something wasn't right. She came home and told me, 'Ted says something shady's going on at the shelter.' Like that."

"Do you think she was referring to the finances?"

"I don't know. I don't think she knew. Just that Ted was uneasy. I didn't pay much attention. This Ted was like a character in a book. I heard about him on Fridays. The rest of the week I never thought about him. But I guess Ted knew what he was talking about."

When he was in the vehicle again, Neil quickly told Kate what he had learned. "Joey Bolduc and Emily Rood are the detectives investigating the animal shelter embezzlement. I suppose I should back off and see what they can do with this case."

"But the murders," Kate said.

"Yes. We're right on the verge of connecting this Burton character to our two murders. It's looking like one big case." Neil sighed. "I'm supposed to be off-duty this weekend. I guess I should let them do some legwork. They're trying to run Burton down and recover the money."

"Will they be able to do it?" Kate asked.

Neil grimaced. Privately, his opinion of Joey Bolduc wasn't stellar. Joey was temperamental and occasionally sloppy in his work.

"They'll keep an eye on the airport, I suppose," Kate said.

"But Burton probably got in his car Friday and drove south before anyone even knew he'd emptied the society's bank account."

"In which case, you can't do much about it," Kate pointed out. "I don't intend to work this weekend unless something incredible happens. But on Monday, I'd like to do another follow-up on this case."

Neil nodded. "I can't let you put it in print that we think Burton is mixed up in this. If he's out there, we don't want him to know we consider him a murder suspect."

"That's what I figured."

"But a lot can change by Monday." Neil started his truck.

On Sunday, Neil again sat with Kate in church. She noticed the looks other women sent their way. She found it mildly amusing and wondered if she was dashing half the female parishioners' hopes.

Adrienne had stayed home with the baby, but extended a lunch invitation to Neil through Connor. Kate realized she was becoming very comfortable around Neil again, and she still wasn't sure that was a good thing. She still wanted to focus on her career. Even if Neil's reformation was genuine, did she want to get serious about a police detective? Neil was as passionate about his work as she was hers. She had to admit, the attraction was still there. Was his faith real? Would he make a good husband and father? And did she want a husband and potential father for her children at this stage in her life? She hadn't settled those questions yet. Seeing him hold Matthew on his lap during the sermon didn't help matters. He looked perfectly at ease, and Matthew snuggled into the crook of his arm as readily as he did with Connor. Neil looked…paternal…confident…content…great.

Adrienne put Matthew and Hailey down for a nap after lunch, and Connor stretched out on the living room sofa with the Sunday paper. Kate took Neil into the study and pulled up the Animal Protection Society's Web site on Adrienne's computer.

"Here's a picture and profile of Jim Burton. I'll print it for you."

Neil studied Burton's thin face: a rather unremarkable man in his middle forties, with light, thinning hair, blue eyes and glasses.

"Family man," Neil mused as he skimmed the bio. "Wife, Claire, and three children, ages twenty-two, nineteen and fifteen. Came here three years ago from New Jersey, where he'd run a nonprofit organization for two years. Before that he was a management consultant." He looked up at Kate. "Why did he take off last Friday? Why didn't he wait another week or two until after the big fund-raiser?"

"Maybe he did intend to wait, but some old people who hung around the shelter got wise to his scheme," said Kate.

"Edna and Ted. You may be right."

Kate leaned back in her chair and watched him. "Do you find weekends annoying?"

Neil looked up at her, his dark eyes wide with curiosity. "I love weekends."

"Sometimes I wish I could work every day."

His lips skewed a little. "I don't know, Kate. That can be dangerous. You need to relax, you know."

"I guess."

"You're excited about your new job. After a while, the novelty will wear off. I know sometimes it's hard to leave it at the office. Like this case we're working on. It started on a weekend—and Christmas Day, to boot—and we seem to keep learning stuff on weekends. But you can't push yourself all the time."

Kate wondered about that. It was true that she wanted more than anything right now to excel at her job. Her early successes had fanned the flames of that desire. She knew that no reporter could have a front-page story every day. Yet, if she were totally honest, she wanted that. She squeezed her lips together, thinking about it. "Do you think I'm selfish?"

Neil raised his head and looked at her keenly. "Well…aren't we all? Especially at—what, twenty-three?"

"Twenty-four," Kate replied. "I'm wondering how other people see me."

"I can tell you that. They see that you're smart, savvy, good-looking and you have a great job that you're good at. I'm sure a lot of people would say you've got it all together."

"That's what I want them to think."

"Don't you feel that way inside?"

She looked down at her hands. "Not really. I'm scared to death every day that I can't live up to what I did last week. Oh, don't get me wrong. I love it that the boss is happy with my work and everyone at the office is congratulating me and telling me what a great reporter I am. But the truth is, I was in the right place at the right time. And if I weren't a detective captain's sister-in-law, I wouldn't have had the success I've enjoyed the past eight days."

Neil nodded. "I can understand that. People have expectations that you're afraid you'll never meet. You make one clever move and they think you're a genius. You're born with good looks, and they assume you're a social mastermind." He added quickly, "Oh, not you. I'm talking about myself. But you must have noticed how that works. The cute little girls get away with a whole lot more than the ones who aren't as cute. I know I was spoiled—the oldest, the only boy. And now I'm twenty-eight, and I know my folks are disappointed."

"How are they disappointed in you?" Kate asked. His words surprised her, but she could tell he was serious about wanting to please his parents.

Neil sighed and shook his head slightly. "I should be married and own a house and have two-point-five kids by now. I should be on a fast track to becoming police chief—"

"Aren't you?" Kate asked.

He smiled at that. "And my faith. My parents were stunned when I became a Christian. That is—when I accepted what Christ did on the cross. They think all Alexanders are Christians because they're 'good people.' But I wasn't, and I don't think they are, either. They get all defensive when I bring it up, and it's gotten so that if I even mention Christ now, they shut down on me."

"Wow." Kate sat still. Her own immediate family members were all believers. Neil must agonize over his loved ones.

After half a minute of silence, he said, "Sorry. I didn't mean to depress you."

"That's okay. I think the Lord wanted me to hear that. Neil, I've been so wrapped up in this job, I haven't been thinking about other people. I've told myself it was only to give my employer what he's paying for, and to do my best—you know, work ethic and all that. But…" She didn't like what she felt at that moment. Had she become a self-absorbed blob of ambition? When was the last time she'd shared her faith with another person?

"Tell you what…" Neil reached over and took her hand in his. "Let's forget about the murders and my folks and the newspaper for today. When Matthew gets up from his nap, let's take him sledding in the park."

As she watched him, a spark lit in Kate's heart. His animation and boyish enthusiasm caught hold of her. "You have a sled?"

"No, but Connor and Adrienne have a toboggan."

"That sounds great. And, Neil?" Kate's eyes locked with his. "Thank you."

Joey Bolduc staggered off the elevator and into the Priority Unit Monday morning. "Man, this better be good, calling me in an hour early."

"Sit down, Joey. New Year's Day was Saturday," Connor said mildly.

"Yeah, well, I missed New Year's Eve thanks to this lousy case, so Roxanne and I made up for it last night." He flopped down in the chair Neil pulled over from Tony's desk. "What do you need?"

"Where's Burton?" Neil asked.

"Not in Maine."

"How do you know?"

"Come on, he stole more than a mil. His wife is distraught. She can't believe he ran out on her and the kids."

Neil raised his hands in exasperation. "Did you find out anything at all this weekend? Did he take a plane?"

"Not under his own name. Why?"

Neil slowly laid out the convoluted path of the Priority Unit's investigations into the Riley and Hepburn murders.

"So you're thinking Burton had something to do with these two kitten huggers being whacked?" Joey asked.

"Makes sense to me," said Neil. "We're thinking that maybe one or both of the victims knew something about his plans. If Burton found out they knew, he may have pushed up his time-table a little. There was going to be a big fund-raising event at the shelter on January fourteenth. If he'd waited that long, he might have gotten away with a lot more."

"But he didn't. He acted on New Year's Eve," said Joey.

"Correction," Neil said. "He started acting on Christmas Day."

"Meaning?"

"Burton planned to liquidate the building fund and take it along with the receipts from the big Fur Ball on the fourteenth. Probably he was planning to abscond with the money that night."

"Abscond?" asked Joey.

"Look it up," said Connor. He winked at Neil.

Neil continued. "But then, along about Christmas Eve, he realized someone was onto his plans. Two old people. He could either shut them up or take off earlier than planned. He chose to shut them up that weekend. It was worth another quarter of a mil if he waited for the proceeds from the ball."

Joey seemed to try hard to make his brain function. "So he bumped off your two victims…."

"Yep," Neil said.

"And took a potshot at a cat."

Neil gritted his teeth. That didn't fit in with his scenario. He shrugged. "Well, anyway, with the two witnesses out of the way, he thought he'd be safe until the Fur Ball. But then something else made him panic. He had to make his move early or never. So he did it. He had the bank transfer funds to another bank, and then had that one transfer them somewhere offshore. And he took off Friday."

"Thursday," said Joey. "His wife reported him missing Friday, but she said he didn't come home Thursday. And the people at the shelter said he left there at noon Thursday and didn't come back."

"So what have you and Emily been doing to try to find him?" Connor asked.

"Checking with all his friends and associates, checking transportation outlets."

"His car isn't missing?" Neil asked.

"No, it was found in the parking lot at the restaurant he lunched at on Thursday."

"So you know where he ate lunch?"

"Well, none of the staff actually remembers him eating there, but they were very busy."

Neil said, "You'd think the waitress would remember if you showed her his picture."

"Nobody remembered," said Joey.

"So maybe he just ditched his car there and hopped a cab to…where?" Neil asked.

"We've checked all the cab companies in town," said Joey. "Nothing. Ditto the airport and bus station."

Connor turned his chair a little and tapped his fingers on his desk. "Someone picked him up."

"Does this guy have a girlfriend?" Neil asked.

"No, he's married."

"I know, I know. But does he have a girlfriend?"

Joey looked blank.

"Find out," said Connor. "Ask his wife—"

"You think his wife would know?" Joey asked, incredulous.

"Stranger things have happened. Ask his wife, all the people at the shelter, the guys he had two-martini lunches with, the Rotarians and the Lions."

"Rotarians?"

"He belonged to the Rotary and the Lions Club," Connor said. "Haven't you done a profile on this guy? You should have done a superdeluxe background check."

Joey looked embarrassed. "We—I figured he got away and there wasn't any point in doing all that. I put out an alert on the national database, but I really don't expect to hear anything."

"Well, that's where you're wrong," said Connor. "We are going to find this guy." He picked up his telephone receiver and punched in an extension number. "Ron? Connor Larson. I learned this weekend that my two homicides are connected to the animal shelter embezzlement case. Detective Bolduc is telling me they have no leads on this Burton who took the money. I'd like my unit to take a crack at it. Would you be okay with my asking the chief to transfer the Burton case to Priority? I think we can do something with it." He listened for a minute, then said, "Yeah, well, I'm positive. Both our victims volunteered at the shelter. I think they were onto Burton, and he went after them. Uh-huh. Yes, I do. Okay."

He hung up and dialed again. Neil just sat and watched him in action.

"Chief? Good morning!" Connor quickly briefed Mike on his unit's discoveries and his conversation with Ron Legere, the detective sergeant.

From the corner of his eye, Neil could see that Joey was sweating it, but trying to act nonchalant.

Connor hung up smiling. "Joey," he said thoughtfully, "you got a break. The Burton case is now ours. You don't have to worry about it anymore."

"Good riddance." Joey stood up. "Don't know why you're so happy about it. They're not going to send you to the Bahamas to find that guy." He sauntered to the elevator and punched in the security code.

"What now?" Neil asked.

"I'm headed to church to thank the Lord for answering our prayers and giving us a break. We're going to get this guy."

"Let's be thankful you didn't pick Joey for the Priority Unit, too," Neil said with a grin, and the two men headed out of the station.

SEVEN

Sergeant Legere gave the Priority Unit the records his men had collected on the embezzlement case. Neil compiled a thick folder containing responses to the sketch of the cat shooter.

"Forty-seven people have called in since the sketch was released," he said.

"Any duplicates?" Connor asked.

"A few."

Neil skimmed each report and made a list of the callers and the person each caller thought the sketch looked like. Number twelve was Stephen Burton.

"Not our guy. Ours is James Burton—same last name." He dog-eared the corner of the report.

"Doesn't James Burton have a son named Stephen?" Connor asked, reaching for a file folder.

Number twenty was also Stephen Burton. In all they came up with four Stephen Burtons and two Eric Robertses. The rest were all different.

"Amazing how people can think a drawing looks like over forty different guys."

"Get photos from DMV," Connor replied.

On his computer Neil went to the state's Department of Motor Vehicles link and searched for a driver's license. He came up with seven Stephen Burtons in the state. One lived at Jim Burton's address. He was nineteen years old.

Neil squinted at the screen. "He looks sort of like the sketch. Want to go for a ride, Connor?"

When they arrived at the Burton residence Claire Burton, Jim's wife, answered the door.

"I thought Detectives Bolduc and Rood were investigating," she said.

"They were, ma'am," said Connor, "but now the case has been transferred to the Priority Unit."

"Well, good. I hope you'll listen to me." She opened the door wide.

"Of course, ma'am. What would you like to tell me?"

"That Jim didn't steal that money. He wouldn't." She closed the door and faced them. "We were very close, and I can tell you, he's not like that."

"Well, it's been confirmed that he emptied the shelter's bank accounts Thursday morning, ma'am. The bank had security videotapes of him withdrawing the money, and a copy of his written request for a transfer of funds from the account."

"That may be. He might have been ready to start paying for the construction on the new building."

"But he and the money are gone, Mrs. Burton."

"So somebody found out how much money he was carrying and stole it from him."

Connor sighed. "Ma'am, he didn't have the money in cash. It was transferred electronically to another bank. We have people trying to trace it and find out the final destination, but we're pretty sure it's not in the U.S. And he abandoned his car at a restaurant."

"What if that wasn't his choice?"

"You think someone kidnapped him and forced him to raid the bank accounts?"

"It's a theory." She folded her arms across her chest and raised her chin.

"Did he have a passport?" Connor asked.

"Yes. Detective Bolduc took it."

"So he had a passport, but he left it here?" Connor was skeptical.

"Yes. He wasn't trying to leave the country, I'm telling you."

"He might have had false ID."

"I don't believe that."

"Well, Mrs. Burton, this isn't really what we came to talk to you about," said Connor.

"What did you come for?"

"Did your husband own a gun?"

She looked startled. "Yes. A pistol."

"How long did he have it?"

"He bought it shortly after we moved up here from New Jersey. There had been several break-ins in the neighborhood."

"Where did he keep it?"

"I'm not sure. In his desk, I think."

"May we take a look?"

"Yes, I guess so."

Connor kept talking to her while Neil searched Burton's desk. There was no gun, but he did find a folder of receipts, and in it, among about a hundred other slips of paper, was a handwritten receipt for a .22 handgun, and it had the serial number on it. Neil took that to Connor and asked Mrs. Burton if he could go through her husband's dresser and closet. On the top shelf of the closet, he found a box and a half of .22 rimfire ammo, but no gun. He picked up the boxes with his handkerchief and took them out to the living room.

Connor was looking at family pictures and saying, "So this is Linda, and these are Sean and Steve?"

"That's right. Linda's married and lives down in New Jersey. She has a little girl."

"And the boys live at home?"

"Yes."

He looked up, and Neil held up the ammunition. Connor came over and looked at it. "No weapon?"

"Nope."

"Keep the boxes. We'll want to dust them for prints." He turned to Claire Burton. She was pouring herself a glass of gin.

"Ma'am, Detective Alexander has found some ammunition for your husband's gun, but not the gun. Could we make a more thorough search for it?"

"Well, I…I guess so. Do you think he took it with him?"

"Actually, I don't," said Connor, "but we have to be sure it's not in the house."

"All right."

"Mrs. Burton, where are the boys now?" he asked.

"Sean is in his room, I think, and Steve is at his girlfriend's."

"He's the older one."

"Yes, he's nineteen." She looked scared now. "Is something wrong?"

"We just need to look for the gun now."

Neil made a careful search with Connor working beside him while Mrs. Burton sat in the kitchen drinking gin.

They entered the older boy's room. There were clothes and books and magazines everywhere, and assorted other junk. Neil pulled the bed apart, then dove into the closet. It was pretty messy. Connor systematically piled up all the things on the floor, then went through the dresser.

"No contraband but cigarettes," he said.

"Connor." At the bottom of the basket of dirty laundry, Neil had found a leather holster. It was empty.

"Bag it."

The fifteen-year-old was standing in the doorway. "Are you guys cops?"

"Yes, I'm Detective Alexander. You must be Sean."

"Yeah, what are you doing?"

"Your mother gave us permission to search the house," Neil said.

"Cool. Want to search my room?"

Neil handed the evidence bag to Connor. "Sure, Sean. What should I look for?"

He laughed a little and walked across the hall with Neil, who opened his dresser drawers, looked under the bed and opened the closet door.

"Aren't you going to look under the mattress?" Sean asked.

Neil lifted one corner. "What's this?"

"My journal. I hide it there so my mother won't find it."

"First place she'd look," Neil said. "Okay, kid, you're clean. Do you know where your father kept his gun?"

"Sure, in his closet."

"Did you ever use it?"

"No, he told me never to even think about touching it."

"Did you?"

"No, I never did. Honest."

Neil eyed him thoughtfully. "How about your brother?"

"Steve? I don't think so." Sean looked as if he might swear or cry any second. "Is my dad really in South America?"

"I don't know. We'll do our best to find him."

"Detective Bolduc said we'd never see him again," Sean said. "He doesn't want to be found."

"What do you think?"

Sean turned away. "My mom says somebody kidnapped him or—or killed him." He swung around and faced Neil. "Do you think he's alive?"

That one was easy. Neil looked the kid straight in the eye. "I do. I really do."

Kate prayed all the way to the newspaper office that morning. She still felt the urge to perform well, but that was now tempered with a strong, steady desire to please God.

Lord, show me what You want me to work on today. If it's a boring zoning board meeting, I'll cover it gladly as the task You've given me.

The answer to her prayer was unmistakable. A sticky note on her monitor read "Please come to my office as soon as you arrive. John C."

She put her coat and purse away and walked with trepidation down the hall to the city editor's office.

"Kate, I'm glad you're here. I expect you're still working on the murder stories, but the news on those has slowed down a lot, hasn't it?"

"Actually, my sources feel things may be breaking soon. But if there's something else you need me to work on…"

"Barry Patterson went skiing last weekend, and he broke his leg. Compound fracture."

Kate frowned. "I'm sorry to hear that."

"You and me both. His doctor says he'll be out at least six weeks. And this Animal Protection Society story is huge. I thought maybe I'd put you on it. The intern might be able to handle Barry's usual school board beat, but…"

She couldn't help grinning. "Oh, thank you, Mr. Cleeves. There's no story I'd rather pick up."

She dashed back to her desk and called the police station. After she'd waited a couple of minutes, the dispatcher transferred her call to the detectives' unit.

"Detective Bolduc," said a sleepy voice. "How may I help you?"

"This is Kate Richards with the *Press Herald*. I'd like to talk to you about the embezzlement case at the animal shelter."

"Can't."

"I…" Kate faltered and cleared her throat, then regained her confidence. Project confidence! "I understood you were the investigating officer."

"Yeah, the key word being *were*. That case was turned over to the Priority Unit this morning. You'll have to talk to Captain Larson or Detective Alexander."

Kate closed her eyes for an instant. *Thank You, Lord!*

A quick call to the Priority Unit told her that Neil and Connor were both out of the office. Kate hung up and drummed her fingers on her desktop. They were out working on the case. She wished the secretary had spilled their location, but Connor had probably trained her not to reveal stuff like that. She'd better not call either of the guys on his cell phone. Instead, she decided to stop by the animal shelter and see if she could pick up any news there and then drive to the police station in person. Maybe when they came back in, she could get the lowdown from Neil. The now-familiar rush of excitement washed over her. She smiled and grabbed her purse.

Connor asked Mrs. Burton for Stephen's girlfriend's name and address.

"We're going over there," he told her. "I'd really appreciate it if you didn't call Stephen or anything. Just let us go over and talk to him."

"You think he did something?" She'd drunk enough gin that Neil didn't think her brain was functioning at its best.

"I don't know, ma'am, but the holster was in his room, and the weapon is missing. I think maybe Steve can tell us where it is." Connor smiled at her. "Maybe he can tell us if his father took the gun with him."

"Think she'll call him?" Neil asked, as they drove toward the girlfriend's house.

"Pray that she doesn't."

The girlfriend's mother let them in, pointed them toward the family room and disappeared. Steve and Alicia were watching TV, and Stephen jumped up off the sofa when Connor walked in holding up his badge and said, "Portland P.D. Just relax, Steve, I'd like to ask you a few questions."

Alicia stood up, looking scared. She wasn't more than sixteen.

"I didn't do anything," said Steve.

"I didn't say you did. I was wondering if you could tell me where your father's .22 pistol is."

Alicia looked from Connor to Steve, then at Neil.

"Why don't you go have a chat with your mom?" Neil said to Alicia with a smile. The girl quickly left the room.

"I don't know what you're talking about," said Stephen.

The sketch wasn't really a good likeness, Neil thought. The young man wasn't bad-looking, but he had an attitude that sapped his appeal. He would probably curse her out if his mother told him to clean up his pigsty of a room.

Connor sighed. "I don't want to waste my time here. Just cuff him and bring him in." He turned toward the door.

"Hey, wait," Stephen cried. "You're going to arrest me because I don't know where the gun is?"

Connor swung around. "No, because you *do* know where it is and you're lying. We found the holster in your room and the ammo boxes with your prints all over them." They hadn't actually run the prints yet, but Neil figured Connor was right. "Now, you can talk about it here, or my pal will handcuff you and read you your rights and bring you to the station. You're going to end up there anyway, so I figure Neil might as well do it now."

Connor left the room that time. He didn't usually do that, and Neil was sure part of it was to intimidate the kid, but Connor was probably sick of the attitude, too.

"Talk," Neil said.

Steven grimaced and looked at the floor.

"Put your hands on your head, then."

Stephen looked at him as if he were nuts.

"This is for real," Neil said. "You're under arrest. Put your hands on your head."

Neil booked Stephen Burton and then took fingerprints off the ammunition boxes and holster while the young man stewed in the lockup downstairs. His next task was to obtain a copy of Jim Burton's prints. He contacted the police department in the New Jersey city where Burton had lived and got codes for access into their arrest records from the time Burton lived there. Sure enough, Jim had been arrested four years earlier for operating under the influence. Neil wondered if the Animal Protection Agency had done a background check on him before hiring him.

"Got anything?" Connor asked as he returned from a meeting with the police chief.

"Jim Burton's prints are all over the ammo boxes and the holster," Neil reported, "but his son Steve's were on the holster, too, and the partially used box of ammo."

"Did you check the serial number of the guns?"

"Yeah. The serial number I found in Jim Burton's desk matches the gun that was found in the Dumpster."

"Perfect. Go log the gun out of Evidence. I'll bring Stephen up here for a little chat."

When Neil returned with the weapon a few minutes later, Kate Richards was seated beside his desk.

"Hey, what brings you here?" He couldn't control the smile that broke across his face. Seeing Kate on a Monday morning was as good as getting an unexpected day off.

"God works in mysterious ways," she said. "In addition to updating the murder story, I've also been assigned to cover the scandal at the animal shelter."

"Then we're working on the same cases. I can live with that."

"Me, too."

Funny how Kate's smile could send him into a tailspin. Focus, Neil!

"It may be a little while before I can talk to you. Connor's bringing a prisoner up here for questioning. Do you want to come back later, or would you like to wait?"

"May I?"

Neil hesitated. They didn't usually conduct questioning with civilians in the office. "I guess so. You can't listen to the session. Privacy rights and all that. But there's a pot of coffee in our break room. Shouldn't be more than half an hour, and I may have something hot for you after we talk to this guy."

Her blue eyes glittered. "Sure. I'll disappear, and you come tell me when the coast is clear."

Seconds after she went through the door to the break room, Connor and Stephen got off the elevator. The Priority Unit didn't have a cell, but it did have a small interrogation room in its office area, and the detectives found it much less hectic than trying to do business downstairs. Neil went inside and started the video recorder, and Connor brought young Burton in and sat opposite him at the table. Connor stated his name and the date of the interview and had Stephen give his name.

"All right, Steve," Connor said pleasantly, "let's talk. Tell me about the gun."

"I don't know where it is."

Connor smiled. "But I do. It's right here." He produced the gun in an evidence bag and laid it on the table. Stephen's eyes bulged.

"Don't you read the paper?" Connor asked. "We found the gun in a Dumpster three blocks from where the cat was attacked."

"What cat?"

"Mrs. Sargent's tiger cat. You shot at it last Thursday. Was that just target practice, or what?"

Stephen eyed him belligerently. "Don't I get a phone call or something?"

"Look," Connor said, "if you want, you can make a call. But I'll warn you, we're not going to set bail. This is a double homicide case. You're not going anywhere today."

Stephen's hands shook, and he clasped them together on the table. "Murder? I didn't shoot anybody!"

"Oh, not even the cat?" Connor's penetrating gray eyes drilled him.

"Fine, I did shoot at the cat," Stephen mumbled.

"Now we're getting somewhere," said Connor. "Tell me about it."

Steve sighed and sat back. "I saw my dad cleaning his gun one night." Connor was silent. Stephen rubbed his eyes. "After he went downstairs to eat breakfast Thursday, I just went and got it."

"You took it out of the closet?"

"Yeah."

"Why?"

He hesitated, then said, "I thought maybe I could sell it."

Connor raised his eyebrows.

Stephen said quickly, "I thought I'd just try it to see if I could make it work first."

"So you got some shells out of the box?" Connor asked.

"Yes. Then I went for a walk. I had it in my pocket."

Connor just waited.

"I went over to Hayner Woods. I thought maybe I'd go down behind there, where there's some woods, and I could take a shot or two. And then…this cat just came walking out in front of me on the sidewalk." He looked up, as though trying to make the detectives see that it was reasonable. "There weren't many houses, and there were no people around, no cars. I just aimed at it and shot. I don't think I hit it."

"You did," Connor said.

"I don't remember. I just know that this lady came running out of the house yelling, 'What are you doing? What are you doing?' And I took off."

"And you threw the gun in the Dumpster."

"Not then," Steve said. "I went home, and I was scared she had called the police."

"She had."

Steve lowered his chin onto his chest. "I hid the gun. I wanted to put it back in my dad's room, but my mother was in there, and I had to go to my job that afternoon."

"Where do you work?"

"A pizza place on Market Street."

"Then what?"

"Friday a friend of mine told me two policemen had been to his house with a drawing, asking people if they knew this guy. He said it looked a little like me, but not really. I got scared, and I went home and got the gun and rubbed it all over with a towel." He looked up. "I wasn't sure that would work. But anyway, I took it back over near Hayner Woods where there's apartments, and I tossed it in a Dumpster."

"Tell me again when you took the gun out of your father's room," Connor said patiently.

"Thursday morning."

"Now, Steve, this is important. You took the gun before your father left the house Thursday."

"Y-yes."

"Did he go back upstairs?"

"I think so, just for a minute. To get his briefcase or something."

"And that's the last time you saw him?"

"Yes." He looked down at his hands. "He didn't come home that day."

Connor tapped his fingers on the table for a few seconds. "And to whom did you think you could sell this gun?"

Stephen's mouth took on a stubborn set.

"Tell me," said Connor. "I'll find out anyway, and if you don't tell me yourself it will go a lot tougher on you."

Sometimes kids bought that line. Stephen did. "This guy I work with, Anthony, he says he knows someone who will buy guns anytime."

"You got a name?"

"No, I was going to ask Anthony."

"And what do you need the money for so badly?"

Stephen closed his lips in a tight line.

"All right, we're going to take you downstairs," said Connor. "The patrol sergeant down there will help you with your phone call. If you want to call your mother, that would probably be best. She can call a lawyer."

If she's sober enough to call one, Neil thought.

He took Stephen down in the elevator, and the patrol sergeant met them and took custody of Stephen. When Neil got back upstairs, Connor was on the phone and Kate was sitting near his desk, listening.

"Right, we can keep him if you think we ought to. Cruelty to animals. We could charge him with stealing his father's gun, I suppose. Well, if you let him bail out, just impress on him and his mother that he needs to stick around and be cooperative." He hung up and said, "That was Crawford, from the D.A.'s office. He's sending someone over. You hungry?"

The question included both Neil and Kate. Neil realized it was almost noon.

"Sure. Maybe Kate would join us at the diner, and you can decide how much we can tell our friendly representative of the *Press Herald*."

EIGHT

An hour later, Kate drove back to the newspaper office. A cold rain was falling, and she shivered as she ran across the parking lot to the door. But nothing could dampen her excitement as she wrote up the story.

Stephen Burton, son of the man who had embezzled the animal shelter's building fund money, had confessed to shooting a woman's cat. It was good copy. The detectives were not yet ready to reveal that the gun Stephen used to wound the cat was also the murder weapon in the two recent homicides, but it would raise all sorts of questions in the readers' minds. Friday night she'd written up the story saying they'd found the gun used in the murders. If they wanted to continue to keep the link to the cat's wounding quiet, that was all right with Kate. Of course, other reporters would pester Connor and Neil, wanting more information. But she felt she was one step ahead of her peers, and with God's blessing.

When she left work at five o'clock, the temperature had dropped below freezing and the streets were slippery. She drove slowly to Gray Goose Lane in the early darkness, giving herself extra room to stop at each traffic light.

Adrienne had meat loaf, baked potatoes and green beans waiting. As they ate in the kitchen, the drumming of rain on the roof of the breezeway changed to pattering sleet.

"I'm glad you're staying with us now, Kate," Adrienne said. "I know you're home safe."

After supper, Kate went to look out the living room window.

The street was a sheet of ice. Power lines glittered like Christmas garlands, and tree limbs were bowed down everywhere in shimmering arches.

"So, today we try to track Jim Burton down?" Neil asked Connor the next morning.

"I think so. Gonna be tough."

"He's already made some mistakes."

It rained and froze, rained and froze all day. The dispatcher called in reserve officers to help with all the collisions. Power lines started snapping that morning, and some companies put the word out for their employees to stay home. The rural areas were hit hardest, with trees going down on the wires. Thousands of people to the north of Portland were without power.

At the station, Neil opened the report Joey Bolduc had made the first day he investigated the embezzlement. He had interviewed the bank manager and obtained a copy of the Animal Protection Society's bank statements. The other detectives reported in for the day while he perused them. A few minutes after eight, Neil and Connor went up to the chief's office.

Mike's secretary, Judith, eyed them solemnly when Connor opened the security door. She was sixtyish and gray-haired, Mike's legacy from the former chief.

"Good morning." She buzzed Mike on the phone. "Captain Larson and Detective Alexander are here." She nodded at them. "Go right in, gentlemen."

Both Police Chief Mike Crowley and Deputy Chief Jack Plourde waited for them. Neil felt a little out of place. They were all wearing suits, even Connor. Neil had on a striped cotton shirt and gray slacks. He kept a jacket and tie in his locker, but avoided wearing them when possible. He mostly kept them handy for when he had to appear in court.

Plourde was younger than Mike, in his late forties, and had curly, light brown hair and steel-rimmed glasses. Connor let Neil fill the brass in on the progress the unit had made on their cases.

"So we've got the son, Stephen Burton, in custody, but he'll probably walk this morning," Neil concluded. "We've got the weapon that was used in the two homicides. I'm pretty sure Jim Burton did it, but we need proof."

"You say he left his passport behind?" asked Mike.

"Yes. His last trip abroad was three years ago, to England. I'll check with Washington to see if he's applied for any visas, but I think it will be a waste of time."

"Joey Bolduc and Emily Rood checked the airport and bus terminal right away, before we got the case," Connor added. "If Burton used public transportation, it was under an assumed name."

Neil gave him a wry smile. "Maybe his wife is right and somebody bumped him off."

Connor shook his head. "I don't believe that. He planned this for months. He was going to carry through and take the proceeds from the fund-raiser next week."

"I agree," Neil said. "But the shelter volunteers were onto him, or at least Ted Hepburn was. Burton got rid of Ted and Edna, and thought he could hang in there until the money came in from the big dance. Then he got spooked and knew he had to run early, without the extra cash."

"What spooked him?" asked the deputy chief.

"The gun," Neil said. "He kept it after the murders. He was probably going to take it with him. Then his idiot son took the gun out of his closet. Burton went back to his bedroom before he left Thursday morning, and the gun was gone. That would scare a two-time murderer who hadn't ditched the weapon."

"He probably thought someone in the family suspected him," said Deputy Chief Plourde.

"Oh, incidentally," said Connor, "Stephen spun a story about a friend of his at the pizza joint, Anthony, with a gun buyer connection. Wouldn't hurt to have one of Ron's detectives check out that little tale."

"I'll tell him," said Chief Crowley, writing in his pocket notebook. "What's your strategy on finding Jim Burton?"

"The way I see it, there are three possibilities," Connor said. "He either left in a private car with an accomplice who picked him up at the restaurant, he left town some other way under a phony ID or he never left town."

Neil stirred, and Mike Crowley nodded at him.

"If he planned this out so far in advance, couldn't he have left another car at the restaurant?" Neil asked.

Connor looked at the city map on the wall. "Yes. My gut tells me there's a woman involved in this."

"Why?" asked Mike.

"A forty-seven-year-old man with a good-looking wife, three kids and a nice house wouldn't leave all that if it meant he'd be on the run alone the rest of his life."

"No previous criminal record?" Jack asked.

"All we found was an old O.U.I. arrest," Neil said.

"You think he built another identity?" Mike asked.

"Had to. At least to get away."

Connor nodded. "I'm going to send my men out this morning to shake down a couple of lowlifes who might have made false IDs for him."

"All right, so you'll try to find out if Burton had false documents. What else?" Mike asked.

"We'll go over his desk at the shelter again," Neil said. "I know Joey and Emily did already, but I like to go through things again when I take over a case. Nothing against those two."

The chief nodded.

"And then I guess we'll plaster his picture everywhere," Connor said, "and I'll immerse myself in Burton data."

Neil knew that meant Connor would go over and over the information they had until something jumped out at him or he went berserk. Neil squinted down at Burton's bank statement in the file he held. "If there was just a way we could keep Burton from getting at that money he transferred."

Connor rubbed his chin. "Maybe we can. If it's not already too late."

"Con, if anyone can do it, you can," Mike said. "Best computer geek I know." He slapped Connor on the shoulder. "All right, you fellows get to work. Keep me posted."

Neil and Connor headed downstairs.

"You think we can find where he had that money sent?" Neil asked.

Connor cracked his knuckles. "I'm sure going to try."

"For what it's worth, I've got an address on that Smith guy you busted for forgery last year. He's got an apartment in the East End."

Connor nodded. "Take Tony and head over there and have a chat with him. I'll see what I can do about these outsourced bank accounts. I used to be pretty good at that stuff."

Smith was definitely nervous when Neil and Tony flashed their badges. He'd been out of prison only three months, and the beads of sweat on his upper lip told Neil he didn't want to go back there. He insisted he was straight now and was holding down a job in a tire warehouse. Neil showed him Jim Burton's picture.

"I heard about that," Smith said. "I didn't do anything for him, believe me. I don't do that stuff anymore, but if I did, I'd remember."

Without a warrant, there wasn't much more the detectives could do. When they returned to the office, Connor stood up and stretched. "I haven't been able to trace the money yet. Neil, I want you and Tony to get to the animal shelter and go over Burton's office with a microscope. Bring me anything that will help me understand him. Jimmy and Lance can go back to the Burton house and go through his desk there. I know you did that, but you were looking for the gun. I need information now."

He sat down at his computer again. Neil and Tony each grabbed a cup of coffee and headed for the stairs.

At noon when they came back, Neil dropped a manila envelope on the captain's desk. "Don't know if it will do any good. Contacts, business associates, appointments he meant to keep this week."

"Great," said Connor. He looked as if he hadn't moved for

two hours, except his tie was loosened and his jacket hung over the back of his chair. "I may be getting closer to finding that million bucks. The good news is, I don't think Burton's actually gotten hold of it yet. That means he probably is still in the U.S. and can't withdraw it until he's on foreign soil."

"So he could still be here in Portland?" Tony's voice held an edge of excitement.

Connor smiled grimly. "Wouldn't that be the icing on the cake? After you get lunch, I'll give you a list of people to interview." He pulled the papers out of the envelope and started scanning them. Neil knew the captain wasn't going to eat.

"I'll bring you a sandwich," he said.

He spent the afternoon chasing down people who knew Burton, but everyone claimed they hadn't known him well. Neil tried discreetly to ask people if Burton had had an extramarital love interest. They were either offended or blasé in their ignorance.

Connor was still at his desk when Tony and Neil returned at the end of the day to start writing their reports.

"Whatcha got?" he called.

"Zilch," Neil replied. "Is Stephen Burton still here?"

"Mrs. Burton bailed him out."

Lance and Jimmy came in from showing Burton's picture to car dealers and car rental agents all afternoon with nothing to show for it. When Neil was ready to leave, he went over to Connor's desk.

"Do you need anything else before I leave?"

Connor looked up from his monitor and blinked. "I've got tomorrow's assignment for you."

Neil looked at him expectantly.

"Think about it tonight, Neil. Burton needs to leave the country, for two reasons. So we won't find him, and so he can withdraw that money. But he can't use his legitimate passport. So, if you were going to make yourself a fake ID, where would you start?"

"Either have a fake driver's license made, or go get someone else's birth certificate to start building a new ID with a real name." That was pretty standard.

"Okay, whose?" Connor looked at him with those stormy gray eyes.

Neil nodded, knowing he didn't want an answer yet. "Go home and cuddle up to your wife and new baby, Connor."

Connor stretched. "Sounds good." He shut his computer down and headed for the locker room.

The next morning Neil took Connor a list of options. He'd thought hard about it the night before. He suggested that the detectives search the homes of the two potential forgers, go undercover on the street to try to locate someone else in the business and check old obituaries for babies who died about the time Burton was born. That last one was a long shot, but sometimes people who wanted a new identity looked up a person their age who had died a long time ago. Anyone could get a birth certificate from Human Services. People doing family histories did it all the time.

Connor read his list, nodding. "Run a check on his family. It would make it a lot easier for him if he could use the identification of someone related to him." He called the other detectives over. "Lance, you're going undercover. Go to this guy Neil spoke to yesterday. His name's Smith, or at least that's one of his names. Tell him you need a new driver's license."

"Am I desperate?" Lance asked. "My license got pulled? How much will I pay to get a new one?"

"We'll go two hundred dollars if we have to," said Connor. "More if you don't have to actually pay him in the end. Don't lie if you can help it."

"Oh, come on, boss. How am I going to do this without lying?"

"You're a very creative person," said Connor. "If he says he'll do it, just tell him you want a license with your picture and another name, and you have cash. I think he'll go for it."

Lance was out the door.

"Tony, you go to Patrick, the guy Lance and Jimmy went to yesterday. Same routine."

"Got it."

"Jimmy, you're going to the courthouse for warrants." Connor wrote orders as he spoke.

It was thirty degrees, and everything shimmered. Roads were slick, and Neil drove carefully around to the Burtons' house. Claire Burton was not happy to see him again.

"Your boss said yesterday you just wanted to talk to Stephen."

"Yes, ma'am, at that point we did," Neil explained, "but we found out Stephen had committed a crime."

"A cat, detective. It was a cat. And the cat will be fine. They said so on the news."

"It's against the law to shoot someone's cat, ma'am."

She started to cry. "This is all connected to the mess Jim is in, isn't it? I still can't believe he took that money. And Stephen isn't a bad boy. He told you he'd never touched that gun before Thursday."

"Yes, ma'am."

She picked up a box of tissues and wiped her face carefully, catching the mascara that smeared beneath her eyelashes. "So what are you here for?"

"Just some information about your husband's family. It might help us find him."

She sat down with Neil at last and told him about her husband's brothers and sister, all the friends whose names she could remember and people he had worked with before coming to Maine.

"Now, Mrs. Burton, please don't get upset when I ask you this," Neil said. "It's just a routine question."

She nodded.

"Did your husband ever have an affair?"

"Of course not!"

"No girlfriends?"

"No! You're insulting me."

"No, ma'am, I'm not. It's just that we have to consider these things."

"Well, he didn't."

"You never wondered?"

"Well, sure, I wondered." She was no longer adamant. "Doesn't every wife wonder?"

Neil hoped his wife never would, when he had one, and that he never gave her reason to wonder, but he didn't say that.

"So, when was the most recent time you…wondered?"

She crumpled the tissue in her hand and threw it toward a wastebasket. Another tear started down her cheek, and she pulled out a new tissue. "Last fall, I guess."

"Was there someone in particular that made you think…"

"It was just a remote possibility. They had the Fun for Pets day at the shelter, and I thought…"

"What, Mrs. Burton?"

"Nothing, really, but he watched her. She had a Samoyed husky, and it really was gorgeous. He placed high on the obstacle course, and Jim went over to congratulate her. But he always speaks to as many people as he can at events for the shelter, makes himself very charming. He raises a great deal of money for them."

"I'm sure he does." She still wasn't getting it. He was raising money for himself. "Does she have a name?"

"Natalie something. She adopted the dog from the shelter, I think. Maybe Roberta Palmer could tell you. But Jim wasn't—" She stopped, shook her head and wiped away more tears.

Neil pulled into the police department parking garage at lunchtime. Connor was getting into his Explorer. Neil walked over quickly, opened the passenger door and stuck his head in.

"You got something?" Connor asked.

"Maybe."

"Hop in. We'll feed you lunch."

On the way to Connor's house, Neil told him about the

woman with the Samoyed. "Roberta Palmer looked up the dog adoption for me. Her name is Natalie DeWitt. Roberta says she's very pretty, very chic."

"Hmm. I wonder if she's single, and if she has a job."

"I can find out after lunch." Neil tried to fish something out of the back of his mind, without success.

"Good," said Connor. "Find out if she's been in her usual territory since Thursday. That's another thing. Check all the recent missing persons cases."

"You think if a woman took off with him, her family would report her missing?"

"If she didn't give a pretty good excuse for dropping off the face of the earth."

"I'll do it."

"So, what about the family? Any brothers that died young?"

"Nope."

"Cousins?" Connor asked.

"Mrs. B wasn't sure, but I have phone numbers for three aunts who may enlighten us."

"All right. Tony got a fake driver's license this morning and arrested Patrick. I had Tony tell him that if he can deliver useful information on Burton, we'll cut him a deal."

"How about Lance's forger?"

"Nope, that guy's either clean or really good at covering his tracks." Connor pulled into his driveway. "You'll all be busy this afternoon, I guess. There are enough leads to last all week."

To Kate's surprise, Neil came home with Connor for lunch. His eyes widened when he saw her setting the table, and he gave her that heart-stopping smile. In that moment, she was very glad she had become part of the Larson household.

"They sent us home early because of the weather," she explained as she got out an extra set of silverware. "I'm working on a story from here, and I'll e-mail it to the editor, but I'm almost done with it."

Connor told Adrienne how boring things were at the office. She could see right through him.

"Oh, sure. You like nothing better than untangling the knots in a tough case." Adrienne tied a bib around Matthew's neck. Dark patches beneath her eyes revealed her fatigue.

At that moment a faint wail came from somewhere in the house. Adrienne turned toward the sound.

"Let me get her," Kate said. She hurried to the bedroom and lifted Hailey from her bassinette. "Aw, you are such a cutie! Come on, let Auntie Kate change you." When she reentered the kitchen, the baby was once more screaming, even though she now had a clean diaper and sleeper suit. "Hey, Hailey," Kate cooed, "don't cry. Uncle Neil is here to see you."

She stooped so Neil could see the baby's face. Hailey actually paused and stared at Neil for a second, then opened her mouth in a loud wail.

"Cute kid," Neil said to Connor over the noise as Kate passed the baby to Adrienne.

"Say that at 2:00 a.m." Connor pulled out his wife's chair.

"No, I'd better go feed her," Adrienne said. "You guys go ahead." It was very quiet when she and Hailey exited.

"Wow. Are you two getting any sleep?" Neil asked.

"Not enough," Connor admitted. "Adri's worn-out." They all sat down, and Connor asked the blessing. When they finished eating, he said, "Excuse us if we eat and run, Kate. I'll just go and say goodbye to Adri."

A thought that had been forming in Kate's mind leaped to her lips. This was the perfect opportunity to get another close look at the investigation. "Hey, I don't suppose you'd take me along this afternoon? I could bring my laptop and work at your office. Then if anything exciting happened, I'd be right there."

Connor smiled and shook his head. "I don't think that's such a great idea, Kate. But I give you points for being the most ambitious reporter I've ever met. We don't let civilians hang around the office without a very good reason."

She regretted speaking up. Here she was, wheedling for a favor that might cause problems for him. "I'm sorry. I've tried not to be so me-oriented lately, but that was pretty selfish, wasn't it? I should stay here this afternoon anyway, so Adri can have a nap."

He shrugged. "I admire people who push hard to excel. And it's not *totally* against regulations. To be honest, the police department is in low gear today. Most of the on-duty officers are out on traffic duty because of all the accidents. I told our unit's secretary to go home after lunch. But…"

"It's okay. Really. And thanks for being honest with me."

Connor winked at her. "Thanks for taking it so well."

She settled down to work in the living room, where she could hear either Matthew or Hailey if they stirred from their naps. Stillness covered the house, except for the clicking of her computer keys.

Shortly after three o'clock, Matthew came down the stairs, still sleepy-eyed. Kate took him to the kitchen for a snack and had just sat down with him for milk and cookies when the phone rang.

"Kate, it's Connor. Sorry to bother you. I think I left my PDA there. I thought I could get along without it, but I can't."

"Where is it?" she asked.

"Either on the kitchen table or the dresser in the bedroom."

"Hold on." She smiled at Matthew. "I'll be right back." She went through the sunroom and tapped on Adrienne's bedroom door.

"Yeah? I'm awake."

Kate pushed the door open. Adrienne sat on the edge of the bed, putting on her slippers.

"Sorry. Connor thinks he forgot his PDA." Kate scanned the dresser top and spotted the fancy cell phone and organizer. She picked it up and went back to the kitchen.

"Found it," she told Connor.

"Great. Uh…"

"Adri's getting up. I could bring this in to you." She added quickly, "I won't stay—just drop it off for you."

"Could you? That would save me some time."

"Sure."

"Thanks, Kate. And drive carefully. The streets are awful."

Adrienne assured her she'd be fine with the children, and Kate escaped into the icy world outside. Always a cautious driver, she took extra pains today and arrived at the police station unscathed. When she entered the Priority Unit's office, Neil was working at his desk to the left. He looked up with a smile and a wave. Connor rose from his desk in a corner to her right.

"Hi, Kate. Thanks for bringing that." He took the phone from her. "How was the driving?"

"A little scary."

"Why don't you have a cup of coffee before you go?" He looked over at Neil. "Could you get Kate a cuppa?"

"Sure." Neil left the room, and Connor gestured toward an extra chair near his desk. "How's Adri doing?"

"She and the kids had a nice nap right after lunch."

"Great."

Tony Carlisle came in from the stairway, stopped in the middle of the office and grinned. "All right! Kate's here. What can we show you today? The AFIS system, maybe?"

Kate smiled at him, but Connor growled, "Get to work, Carlisle." He turned to Kate. "Neil has been making some calls to Jim Burton's aunts."

"His aunts?" She frowned at him, puzzled. "I don't get it. You think his aunts would know where he is?"

"Not exactly. I'll let Neil explain it to you."

Neil came back with two cups of coffee and handed her one. "You want some, Captain?"

"No, thanks. Tell Kate what you're doing, but this is off the record. No way do we want Burton to know what we're thinking."

She nodded. "Sure. Thanks."

Neil led her to his desk and removed several file folders from a chair so she could sit down. "We're trying to find out if Burton has built a false identity. One of the easiest ways to do that is to use the vital statistics of a relative. So I'm contacting his aunts to ask if any baby boys in their family of Jim Burton's generation have died."

Kate thought about that for a moment. "So…if a baby died, he could use the birth certificate?"

"Yes. And if the relative died at a later age, he might have other useful documents, like a Social Security number. Plus, Jim might have been able to find copies of his signature to forge."

"Wow. I never would have thought of that."

"Well, Aunt Number One was kind of upset that her nephew is being accused of criminal activity. She wouldn't give me any information at first, but after we chatted for a while, she gave me a list of Jim's cousins on his father's side. All seventeen of them."

"Are they all still living?" Kate asked.

"No, Stephanie died when she was seven. The rest are still alive."

"Hmm. I guess a girl cousin won't help you."

"Right. The aunt said the only one on that side who died as an infant would be her brother Thomas's wife's miscarriage."

Kate made a face. "That won't help, either."

"Nope. On to Aunt Number Two—Aunt Esther." He picked up his phone.

Apparently, Aunt Esther didn't even want to talk to him.

"No, ma'am," Neil said hastily into the receiver. "I assure you I am not a con artist." He stared at the receiver in disbelief. "She hung up on me."

Kate couldn't help laughing. "Sorry."

"She said anyone could say he was a policeman. Of course, she's right, but she didn't have to slam the phone down so hard."

Kate's private opinion was that if he'd gone to visit Aunt Esther in person, she wouldn't have been able to resist his adorable brown eyes—but she wasn't going there. Or was she? She shook her head to clear it. "Anyone left on your list?"

"There's Aunt Phyllis, Jim Burton's mother's sister. Only

eight cousins on that side, so far as we know." He began dialing while Kate sipped her coffee.

"And are they all living?" Neil asked his contact. "Yes, ma'am, I'd like the dead ones, too. Yes, ma'am, the longer they've been dead, the better." Kate made a face at him, and Neil quickly amended his statement. "I'm sorry. That didn't come out right. What I'm looking for is a boy who was about Jim Burton's age, who has passed on."

This time he ended the conversation smiling. "Guess what, Kate."

"What?"

"Aunt Phyllis's son Joseph died twenty years ago. He'd just gotten out of medical school, and he had a car crash. It was a terrible blow and a huge disappointment to the whole family. So tragic. He was the most promising of all the boys."

Connor had lifted his head and was listening, too. "What's his name, Neil?"

"Joseph Parlin."

"Birth date?"

"He was two months older than Jim," Neil told him. "And you'll love this. His mother still has his birth certificate. She's faxing me a copy."

The fax machine next to the secretary's desk began to hum. Neil and Connor both jumped up and walked over to watch the document print.

"Okay," Connor said. "So he was old enough to have a driver's license and a Social Security card. Let's check it out."

Kate followed them to Connor's desk. Even though she couldn't write this story today, she might be able to use it later.

"Connor's trying to get into the DMV records in Augusta to see if anyone with the name Joseph Parlin has a current Maine driver's license," Neil explained. "But it seems their computer system is down. The ice storm knocked the power out in most of the capital early this morning. If the electrical service isn't restored by morning, all the state government offices will be closed tomorrow."

"Call the nearest Social Security office and see if they're still open," Connor said. "We may be able to bypass Augusta to get the information we want."

Neil went to his desk and made a quick call. "They're open."

"Go get 'em, Tiger. I'll get back to chasing the bank records."

Kate shrank back toward the secretary's desk, stifling the urge to beg them for another favor.

Neil glanced at her, then back at his captain. "Uh, Connor?"

"What?" Connor glanced at him, then focused on Kate. "Look, Neil can't take you along, kiddo, but I know you're dying to go."

"I'm sorry. I won't—"

"If a reporter happens to show up at a venue where a cop is working, that's one thing. Expecting special treatment is another."

"I know." She started to apologize, but stopped and eyed him carefully. "Are you... Uh, I might just have some business down at the Social Security office...."

"Imagine that." Connor slid his reading glasses on and turned back to his computer. Neil grinned at Kate and headed for the stairway. She hurried down the stairs behind him.

NINE

They sat in the waiting area at the Social Security office for half an hour.

"I should have called ahead and talked to the supervisor." Neil rose and began to pace. After another fifteen minutes, his name was called. They were led to a cubicle where a clerk whose name tag read "S. Martin" asked Neil how she could help him. They stood for ten minutes while she searched on her computer for a file under the name of Joseph Parlin.

Neil began to fidget. Finally, the clerk looked up with a smile. "It seems Joseph Parlin's number is active."

"Is there a question?" Neil asked.

"Well, twenty years ago we were notified that he was deceased, and his account was canceled. But recently we received an affidavit saying Joseph Parlin was alive. Apparently, he'd been MIA or something. Some ghoulish mistake, I guess. Anyway, the number was reactivated in…July."

"July." Neil looked at Kate. "He's been planning this since July. Now, tell me, miss, who submitted that affidavit? Because I just talked to Joseph Parlin's mother, and she says he's still dead."

More time on the computer. The clerk moved slowly, hitting a key, then waiting, then hitting another. "His cousin," she said at last.

"James M. Burton?"

"That's correct."

"All right," said Neil, "can you give me Parlin's current address?"

"Do you have authorization from Mr. Parlin?" the clerk asked. "Because I'm not supposed to give out that infor—"

"Mr. Parlin is dead," Neil said patiently. "How am I supposed to get his authorization?"

"I'm sure I don't know, sir."

"I am a police detective," he said carefully, one word at a time. "This is a murder investigation. Isn't that authorization enough?"

She looked confused. "Perhaps you should speak to my supervisor. He's over there." She gestured toward a man in a three-piece suit at a desk noticeably larger than any of the others in the room.

"Good idea, but don't lose your place in that computer, because I'll be right back for that data."

Kate followed Neil to the supervisor's desk. Neil explained the situation and how James Burton, who was now a fugitive, had sworn his dead cousin Joseph Parlin was alive.

"We think Mr. Burton may have assumed his cousin's identity as a way to escape undetected after killing two people and stealing a million dollars from the Animal Protection Society," Neil said.

"I see." The supervisor took off his glasses and started wiping them with a tissue. "A very interesting story."

"Sir," Neil said with his most persuasive smile, "we need to get the current address for Joseph Parlin, that is, the man using the name Joseph Parlin. You need to authorize your clerk to release that information to me."

"Highly irregular," he said skeptically.

"Maybe so, but this is a murder investigation. Do I need a warrant?"

The supervisor eyed him for a moment, put his glasses back on, stood and walked over to the clerk's desk.

"Miss Martin, you may give this gentleman the information he's requested. Just type it out and print three copies. Give them one and place one in the box for—"

Neil gritted his teeth and pulled a small notebook from his breast pocket. "Could you just tell me the address, miss, and then you can type it up after? We really need to get going."

"Seventy-four Hitchings Road, Westbrook," she said.

Neil smiled, wrote down the address and walked out the door.

As soon as they were outside, Kate burst into laughter. "So that's how you get information out of a brick wall. Do you really think Jim Burton is hiding out in Westbrook?"

"I dunno. It's too close, really. Someone could see him anytime." Neil walked her to her car. "Careful. It's icy there. Jim could alter his appearance. You know, contacts instead of glasses, grow a mustache, that kind of thing. And if someone thought they recognized him, he could just say, 'I'm his cousin,' and whip out his driver's license."

"I guess you're right." She smiled up at him. "I'll follow you back into town, but I don't think I'd better go to the police station again. That would be pushing it a little far. I'll head for home."

"Okay. Drive carefully."

"Thanks a lot." She got into her car and started the engine. As she pulled out onto the street, she looked in her rearview mirror and saw Neil standing motionless on the sidewalk, still watching her.

Neil got behind the wheel of his car and slowly made his way back to the station. When he got to the office, he checked with the Department of Motor Vehicles again. Apparently, their power was on, and he was able to get Joseph Parlin's driver's license this time. As Connor came from the break room with a fresh cup of coffee, the image came up on the screen.

"Lousy picture," Connor said. "Print it out."

It was definitely Jim Burton with brown eyes, not blue, and dark hair, full and thick on top. Corrective lenses required, but no glasses. And no record of motor vehicle violations.

Neil studied it for a long moment, then shook his head. "Hard to believe that's the same man."

"Let's get the whole unit together and hash this over," Connor said.

Suddenly the lights went out, the computer screens went

black and the office was still. The big windows on two sides let in the dim afternoon light, so they could still see. Dimmer lights around the edge of the room came on.

"We'll have minimal power if we have to run on generators," Neil said.

The monitors around the room lightened, and all the men went to their desks to reboot their computers. Connor took his cell phone down the hall toward the break room. Neil figured he was checking in with Adrienne.

When he came back a couple of minutes later Jimmy asked him, "Got power at your house, Captain?"

"Nope. It went out when ours did." He called the men to his desk. "All right, it looks like Jim Burton set up an ID under his dead cousin's name and put a Westbrook address on his driver's license and Social Security record."

"Westbrook?" said Lance. "Incredible. He can't still be there."

"You may be right," said Connor. "He set this identity up to shield his getaway, but he'd be stupid to stay there long."

"So, are we going over and check it out?" asked Jimmy.

"You bet. But we've got to get the Westbrook police in on it. You can set that up, Jimmy. Call their day patrol sergeant and fill him in. Ask for a unit for backup. Tony, you go get the warrant. Jimmy and Lance, call home and tell your wives you'll be late for supper and not to worry. Gentlemen, please wear your vests."

They all headed for the locker room.

An hour later, the Priority Unit went back to the city and wearily climbed the stairs. Even if the men had wanted to use the elevator, they couldn't. The generator ran only necessary equipment. There wasn't any hot water in the locker room.

Neil yanked the Velcro on the side seam of his bulletproof vest. "No clothes or furniture in the house. Nothing. What a bust."

"Big disappointment for the captain," Jimmy said as he peeled off his vest.

"Well, we knew it was a long shot that Burton had stayed around," Neil admitted, "but I was hoping."

"We all were," Jimmy said.

Tony hung his jacket and vest in his locker on the other side of Neil's. "I thought we had something, too."

"We did," Neil reasoned. "We still do. And Lance has some information on that woman Natalie, the one with the Samoyed. We can check her out tomorrow. If the Registry of Deeds is open, we'll get data from them and find out if he had financing for the house. There'll be lots of things to do tomorrow. Maybe Connor can even figure out how to make that offshore bank freeze Burton's account."

Connor breezed in from the outer office. "Head on home, men. Neil, are you going to your apartment?"

"Yeah."

"Drive carefully. It's starting to sleet again. Do you have heat at home?"

"I've got a kerosene heater."

"Why don't you just come to the house? We've got the fireplace and a little woodstove in the garage. I can set it up in the sunroom if we need it."

"I'll be okay."

"I'll worry about you dying of carbon monoxide poisoning," Connor admitted.

"I can go to my folks'. They've got a woodstove."

"If you want. But we'd be happy if you came to our house."

It was tempting. Kate would be there. This new friendship with her was definitely a good thing, but he didn't want her to think he was pursuing her again. He was still wary from the way they'd crashed and burned last summer. Still, he hoped any lingering doubts she harbored about him could be resolved as they matured spiritually. And he knew that, for once in his life, he didn't want to blow this relationship.

"I'll be fine," he told Connor.

He drove home and took his flashlight out of the glove compartment, then trudged up to his apartment and went in. It was nearly as cold in there as it was outside. It took him a while to get the heater going. When it was burning in the kitchen, he used bottled water to make himself a glass of Tang, then sat in front of the heater, warming his hands. When they were warm enough, he made a sandwich and ate it.

On impulse, he took out his cell phone. Would the ice storm affect the transmitting towers? He clicked to his phone's address book and stared at the number, trying to decide if he should call or not.

Probably best to leave Kate alone. But he wanted to call her, and hear her voice again. After a long moment, he clicked instead to another number.

"Pastor Robinson? This is Neil Alexander."

The minister's warm voice calmed him, and Neil felt he'd taken the right course. "You said you'd help me study the Bible if I wanted, and there are some things I feel as though I need tutoring on."

"I'd be happy to meet with you once or twice a week. In fact, you'd be welcome here at the parsonage this evening, if you don't mind studying by lantern light."

Neil smiled. "Thank you, sir. I'll be over in a few minutes."

Connor called Neil early in the morning. "We can have showers in the locker room at the station if we get there early, before the shift changes and the generator is on peak use."

Neil scrambled into his clothes and shut off the kerosene heater. He didn't dare leave it running when he wasn't there. He drove to work carefully, passing two fender benders on the way. People were in the park, chopping ice with hatchets and filling buckets. He assumed they would take it home and melt it to wash with. He hoped they wouldn't drink it.

Connor brought two gallons of bottled water to the office.

"Adrienne stocked up before we lost power," he said. "When she heard some areas blacked out, she bought twelve gallons of water and a pile of flashlight batteries and candles and crackers."

"How's the baby doing?"

"Good. We're keeping her bundled up. How about you? Were you warm enough last night?"

"Barely. The landlord told me he's keeping the pipes warm in the basement, but it was pretty chilly in my apartment. If we don't have power tonight, I might visit you."

They hit the showers. The other detectives were at their desks when Neil went out into the office.

Neil and Tony drove to Natalie DeWitt's address. No one responded to the doorbell, but inside, a dog barked. Neil tried calling and got her answering machine. They spoke to two neighbors. She worked, but they didn't know where. Lance's report hadn't told them where she was employed, so they went back to the station.

"Joseph Parlin signed a contract on the house in Westbrook," Jimmy told them. "A payment was due yesterday, but the bank didn't receive it, and the Realtor hasn't heard from him."

Connor sent Tony and Neil to court for Stephen Burton's hearing. The judge decided not to send him to trial. Instead, Stephen got a suspended sentence and probation.

The streets were strangely lacking in traffic as Neil drove cautiously back to the station. Most of the stores were closed, and pedestrians were rare. Road crews were throwing salt and sand everywhere to protect the city from lawsuits. He hated to run his truck through it. The diner near the police station was closed, and they were hungry.

"Taco Bell is open," Jimmy told them. Tony and Neil drove over there. Somehow, the restaurant was in a pocket that still had power. They ordered hot coffee and takeout food and took it back to the office. It was nearly two o'clock. Connor was pacing, so Neil knew things weren't going well.

"What's up?" he asked, handing Connor the extra cup of coffee and burrito he'd brought.

"Absolutely nothing. I can't seem to find anything on this Natalie person." The rigid line of his back spelled frustration.

"Did you do a credit check on her?" Neil asked.

"I tried. The system is pretty much down now."

Neil chewed a bite of his burrito and walked to the window. As he looked out on the glittering street below, sipping his coffee, he decided it was time to call his mother.

"Cornelius Jan Alexander! I was worried about you. Are you okay?" she demanded.

"Yes, how about you?"

"We're fine, and Oma is staying here. The Pines has no heat." Neil's grandmother had been living in a retirement home for several months.

"Mom, do you know a woman named Natalie DeWitt?"

"Natalie? Ha!"

"Ha, what?" Neil asked, wishing he'd paid attention to that niggling memory in the back of his mind sooner.

"She's my cousin Bernard's ex-wife," she said.

"Oh, right, right. She lives in Deering?"

"I don't know where she lives. They've been divorced for ten years. I haven't seen her for longer than that."

"So you don't know where she works?"

"Last I heard, she was a hostess at the Elite Lounge."

"Really?"

"Yes, but she's the type that moves around."

"Does she like dogs?"

"Well…when she was married to Bernie she had German short-haired pointers. Very high-strung dogs. Drove Bernie nuts."

"Thanks, Mom."

"What, this is for work?"

"Well, her name came up. I thought maybe you'd know who she was."

Connor was trying once more to get somewhere with his computer. "I think our Internet provider has closed up shop," he said when Neil stood beside his chair.

"Natalie DeWitt used to work as a cocktail hostess at the Elite Lounge. She may not still be there."

"That's my boy." Connor stood and clapped him on the shoulder. "The reason you know this is…?"

"I asked my mother. I thought I remembered her mentioning Natalie."

"Great! When the florist down the street reopens, I'll send her flowers."

Neil tried to call the lounge, but no one answered.

"Maybe we'll drive by there tonight," Connor said. "Come on. We've got our computers up, but if the provider is down, what good does it do? We may as well go home."

Neil stopped at his apartment to get his things. It was barely above freezing in there. He ate a peanut butter sandwich and got his sleeping bag and pillow and a change of clothes for the next day.

The streets were still hazardous, but with his four-wheel-drive and pursuit driving experience, Neil felt almost invincible. He was going to see Kate again. Every time he thought of her now, anticipation prickled him. She was different from any other woman he'd taken an interest in. Last summer he'd seen that as a drawback, but now he saw her in a different light, and he was sure that was good.

He thought about her as he drove to Connor's house. She was honest about her ambition. If she needed a story for the paper, she said so. And if she just wanted to have fun, like the sledding on Sunday afternoon, she didn't act coy about it. He thought he'd gotten beyond Kate the Reporter and had reached Kate the Friend. He liked that Kate.

When he got to the Larson house and suggested taking Kate out for a perusal of the Elite Lounge, her eyes lit up.

"More investigating," she said eagerly.

But Connor's reaction burst Neil's bubble of confidence.

"First of all, that's not the kind of place I want you taking my sister-in-law."

"Oh, come off it," Neil said. "This isn't a date. We'll just go in and ask for Natalie. If she's not there, we'll leave."

Connor scowled. "Second of all, they're probably closed."

"Are you kidding? Bars are the last places to shut down in an emergency."

"That's right," Kate chimed in, but when Adrienne and Connor stared at her, she scrunched her neck down as though trying to disappear inside her turtleneck sweater. "Of course, I have no personal experience to go by."

"We'll check Natalie DeWitt's house again first," Neil offered. "But from what my mom said, she's the type who works nights. If she's not home, we'll drive to the lounge and just see if she's working tonight."

"All right," Connor said at last, "but Kate stays in the truck at the Elite Lounge."

Neil bristled. "I don't think so. Not in that neighborhood."

Kate walked over to Connor and touched his arm. "Connor, I'm twenty-four years old, and as much as I appreciate you, you're not my father. I'll be safe with Neil."

Yes! She believed in his change. Neil straightened his shoulders.

Connor ran a hand through his short, curly hair. "Sorry. I just don't want the next trauma I'm called to respond on to be you."

"Is this high-risk?" she asked.

"You never know."

"Trust me," Neil said, "walking into a nightclub is not life threatening unless you're in uniform. And the Elite Lounge is a cut above some of the…" He noticed Connor's hoisted eyebrows and stiff spine then and backpedaled. "I mean, in my professional experience. I actually haven't been in there in at least a year. Honest."

Connor frowned, but then threw up his hands. "Go, then. But if you so much as skid into a snowbank, I'll have your hide."

"Right. Absolutely." Neil hustled Kate toward the coat closet. "We should be back by ten."

"You'd better be."

TEN

"Yikes," Kate said when they were in Neil's pickup. "I've never seen Connor so touchy."

"Yeah, well, he's under a lot of stress right now. And when it comes down to it, he knows I've done a lot of less-than-brilliant things in my life."

"Like hanging around nightclubs?"

"Well, that was then, and this is now. I don't miss it."

Kate sat back, tightening her seat belt. Neil drove slowly toward Natalie DeWitt's neighborhood. After a few minutes of silence, he said, "Thanks for trusting me tonight."

One of the last reservations in Kate's heart melted as she gazed at him. He kept his eyes on the icy road, and she studied his profile. What had started as a crush last summer had escalated so fast she'd let her common sense lag behind. A popular, charming, gorgeous man was lavishing his attention on her.

Adrienne had voiced her concerns early. Neil was giving Kate "the rush," and she should be cautious. His reputation was a red flag. Connor had agreed—Neil was a steady detective but a notorious heartbreaker. It would be hard to find a single woman in the police department whom he hadn't dated and dropped.

In only two weeks, Kate had known she'd fallen in love. But Neil never said he loved her. It's too soon, she'd told herself. But he hadn't thought it was too soon for a physical relationship. It was his easy dismissal of her protests that had brought the interlude to a screeching halt. Didn't he care about her convictions? If not, that meant he had no respect for her. The bleak realization had stunned her. She had confronted him, and the tone had turned nasty enough for her to cut short her visit to Adrienne and Connor, returning home hurt, embarrassed and angry at herself for not listening to them or to God's clear guidance.

The Neil Alexander she saw now was not the same man. Could six months make such a vast difference? How long should she hold back, observing critically, before she believed the transformation was permanent? And was that up to her? Only God could see Neil's heart. She didn't want to rush back into a romantic relationship with him, and yet deep down she still longed to be loved by the man she'd once imagined Neil to be. Was he becoming that man now?

He glanced over at her, his dark eyes anxious, and she realized she hadn't responded to his remark.

"If you forgive someone, you can't keep punishing them for what they did. Besides…" Her chest tightened, and she swallowed hard. "What happened last summer wasn't all your fault. I knew I shouldn't date a non-Christian. But when you asked me out, I was so flattered and excited, I didn't care. I'm sorry, too, Neil. I never should have gone out with you. I've confessed that to God, but…will you forgive me, too?"

Neil braked carefully and brought the truck to a halt at a stop sign. He looked over at her in the dim light cast by the instrument panel. "I don't think there's anything to forgive, Kate, but yes. I've straightened that out with God, too. I know I was living the wrong way, and I'm starting to learn the right way. I don't want to hurt anyone ever again."

"Thank you." She blinked away the tears that formed in her eyes and reached over to touch his sleeve for an instant. "I'm glad." She sent up a silent prayer for Neil as he eased the pickup out onto the next street and drove toward Natalie's house.

Ahead of them, a pool of light shone down from a streetlight.

"Hey! This neighborhood has electricity," Neil said.

"That's not fair." She put on a pout, and Neil chuckled.

Lights shone from Natalie DeWitt's windows. He pulled into

the driveway. They walked to the door together, and Neil rang the bell. A few seconds later, it opened a crack.

"Yes?"

No wonder Mrs. Burton was jealous, Kate thought. Natalie's dark hair was pulled back in a ponytail. No gray. Her dramatic makeup showcased a lovely face. Her expression held only a tinge of wariness.

"Natalie DeWitt?" Neil asked.

"Yes."

"I'm Neil Alexander with the Portland P.D. May we come in and ask you a few questions?"

She hesitated and looked beyond him at Kate. Kate tried to look as official as possible. It wouldn't do to have her guessing that the detective had brought a friend along on his investigation.

Natalie stepped back and let them enter, but she didn't offer them a seat.

"Do you know James M. Burton?" Neil asked.

"I...don't think so."

"Have you read about his disappearance in the newspaper?"

"Oh, the animal shelter guy!"

"Right. Do you know him?"

"I've met him. Wouldn't say I actually know him."

"We're trying to locate Mr. Burton. We thought perhaps you could help us."

"Me? That's strange. I've seen him once or twice is all."

"You saw him at the Fun for Pets day?"

"I guess so. I took my dog to that."

"Have you seen him since?"

"I'm not sure. There was another event at the shelter. I may have seen him then."

"So you've never seen him away from the shelter?"

"I don't believe so. Why?" A white, long-haired dog came and leaned against her leg, panting.

"Just part of our investigation, ma'am. Could you please tell me where you're employed?"

"The Spinning Wheel Restaurant. Tonight's my night off."

The dog approached Kate and snuffled her hand. Kate stroked his head. He gazed at her with big blue eyes and yawned. She couldn't help smiling.

Neil asked a few more questions that Ms. DeWitt seemed to answer honestly and without hesitation. Neil thanked her for her time.

"I had high hopes but I don't think she's the one," he admitted to Kate in the truck.

"Burton's wife was imagining things," she said.

"Or Ms. DeWitt's a skilled prevaricator."

"You're a good judge of people."

"Not always." He threw her an oblique glance, as though wondering if he was reading her right.

Kate hoped she was reading Neil's signals right, too. She liked him a lot, but the timing still wasn't good. She'd kept reminding herself all week that now was the time to build her career. Romance could come later. She wouldn't want him to think she only wanted to be around him if he fed her information for her articles. They both needed more time to let the dust settle from last summer before even considering getting involved romantically again.

The power was still out on Gray Goose Lane when they returned. Connor had opened the couch for Neil to sleep on.

"You'll be warmer if you sleep by the fireplace." They lit candles in the kitchen, sunroom and living room. Connor had the woodstove in the sunroom, and he built the fires up in it and the fireplace as soon as Neil and Kate got there.

"I brought my sleeping bag," Neil told Adrienne. "You don't need to get sheets out for me."

"Kate and Matthew slept down here last night, and we shut off the upstairs," said Connor, "but we'll try to warm things up enough so she can be comfortable in her room."

Neil threw a glance Kate's way. "Maybe I should go home."

"Don't do that," Kate said. "I'll be fine. I've got two quilts."

"You'd freeze at your place," Connor said. "Matt's already asleep in our room. He might just stay there tonight." He hung the poker by the fireplace. The downstairs was comfortable by then. They had three pans of ice and snow on the woodstove, melting so they could use it to flush toilets. Connor and Adrienne sat down on the wicker settee in the sunroom. Adrienne had set out bottled water and packaged cookies for a candlelight snack.

"Well, it's too bad Miss DeWitt didn't turn out to be a good lead for us," Connor said.

Neil smiled. "At least we put that rumor to rest without having to go bar-hopping."

Connor was not amused. "Maybe we'll get a break tomorrow. I think once this power crisis is over, the governor will help us get the authority we need to freeze that bank account." He pulled Adrienne against him.

They chatted for a few more minutes, and then Adrienne said, "I think I'll turn in. Not that the company isn't scintillating, but I know Hailey will be up within a couple of hours, and I may as well sleep while she does."

"Probably a good idea for everybody," Connor said. "The chief called and told me the crews are working around the clock to get the power back up. Tomorrow should be a big day to catch up on everything we couldn't do today."

Kate stood and gathered the empty water bottles and cookie package.

"Want to get that candle in the kitchen while you're out there?" Connor asked.

"Sure." She threw away the wrapper and left the bottles by the sink. The one candle burning on the counter barely illuminated the kitchen. Kate bent over and puffed it out. When she went back to the sunroom, Adrienne handed her a flashlight.

"All set?"

"I think so. Thanks."

Connor had already disappeared, and Adrienne headed for the master bedroom. Kate rounded the corner into the living room.

Neil was spreading his sleeping bag on the sofa. The blaze in the fireplace snapped merrily.

"You sure you'll be warm enough up there?" he asked.

Kate smiled. "Yeah." She held her hands toward the fire for a moment. "Seems like a special occasion, doesn't it? My folks hardly ever have a fire in their fireplace."

"It's very special."

"Neil…" She turned toward him. "I'm glad I've had the chance to get to know you again the past couple of weeks."

"Me, too."

She smiled at him, feeling as though she didn't need to learn any more to trust him now.

They stood looking at each other in the soft light for a long moment.

Neil chuckled. "I want to say you're exactly the way I remembered you, but you're not. The truth is, you're better than the woman I hung out with last June. You're deeper than I ever realized, and I think you're more beautiful now."

She felt her face flush. "You're different, too. In a good way. I used to hear Connor talk about this brash, flippant kid he had trained."

"He must have been talking about Tony."

They both laughed.

"Well, that intrigued me. But I think I like you better now." As she looked into his dark eyes and saw the reflection of the fire leaping in them, she knew she needed to keep her distance. Neil was a Christian now, but old habits resurface when the opportunity arises. She hadn't experienced a serious, mature relationship. She'd always figured it would happen when the time was right. Last summer she'd hoped that the time had come and had been disappointed. Was she ready now? And was he?

"I'd better head to bed." She turned on her flashlight and stepped toward the staircase.

"Kate."

She turned back with one foot on the bottom step. He was still by the fireplace, but when he spoke, she could hear his soft tones across the room.

"Do you think we could start over?"

Her heart raced. Decision time. "What do you mean?"

"I haven't gone out at all in the last six months. But now that I've seen you again, I think I'd like to try a new relationship and see if I can get it right. With God's help."

She smiled. About half her resolutions had just been shattered, but she didn't mind.

"The pastor's been showing me some things from the Bible," he went on earnestly. "Kate, will you give me another chance?"

She caught her breath and sent up a quick prayer. *Is this the right time, Lord?* The old uneasiness was gone. "I think…I think I would."

He closed the distance between them in three strides. "What do you think would make a first-rate date?"

None of the places we went last summer, she thought. Aloud she said, "I don't know. Maybe a boat ride around the bay. But not in January. Hmm. Ice skating?"

"Not a fancy restaurant or a swanky party?"

"Neil, I'm a country girl. I grew up on a farm. If you took me to a fancy party, I wouldn't have the wardrobe, and I wouldn't know what to do with my elbows."

He chuckled. "Are you sure? Just talking about it makes me want to take you to some fancy event. I wonder if Tony could get us tickets to the inaugural ball."

She blinked at him. "Inaugural ball? In Washington?"

"No, in Augusta. You know. Tony's uncle. He just got reelected."

Kate sat down on the second step. "Are you telling me that your bozo detective partner, Tony Carlisle, is Governor Tracey's nephew?"

"Well, yeah. I thought you knew. I thought the whole world knew." Neil gulped. "So now I guess you'll want to interview Tony."

She stared up at him, appalled that the identical thought had occurred to her.

"Because Tony doesn't play it up much," Neil went on. "He wants to be treated just like anyone else—no special privileges or consideration in the P.D. He's a little impulsive, but he's a good cop, and getting better. I don't think he'd want to be interviewed. It would just draw attention to him and ruin it for him to do undercover work."

"I can see that. You're right—it wouldn't help at all to plaster his baby face all over the papers." In her mind, she backtracked to their earlier conversation with Connor. "So, Connor wasn't kidding when he said the governor would help him try to freeze Jim Burton's bank account?"

"I wouldn't exactly say that he and the governor are buddies, but they've met several times, and I'm sure the governor will help if he can. If anyone can trace that money, Connor can. But it's very difficult to keep people from accessing it when it's overseas. Connor's connections may be able to lend him some muscle."

She nodded, thinking about it. "Do you know who I'd really love to interview?"

"Tony's uncle?"

She shook her head, smiling. "Your grandmother."

"Oma?"

"Yes. Both my grandmothers are dead, and they both lived in Maine all their lives, anyway. Your Oma grew up in Holland and came over here as a bride, right?"

"Yeah."

"I'll bet she's got some incredible stories to tell."

"She does. I love to get her talking about her childhood."

Kate stood and found herself eye-to-eye with Neil. She leaned back a little, trying to lessen the effect of his gaze. In the dim light, his eyes were the color of dark, purple brown, velvet pansies. Looking into them too long would surely be hazardous.

"That's my idea of the perfect date," she said softly. "Visiting your Oma and talking to her about the canals and the flowers and the castles and artists and…and growing up Dutch. Leaving all that, and finding a new life here without really losing her heritage."

Neil was quiet, but his gaze seemed to gain intensity. His upper lip twitched as though tempted to quirk into a smile. "How about Saturday?"

"Oh, I didn't mean—"

"You didn't?"

She dared to return the blazing stare. "Yes, I did. But I wouldn't push her. If she didn't want me to write about her, I'd just like to talk to her for my own sake, just to hear her tell about it."

He nodded. "I'll fix it with her. And afterward, I'm going to take you to a really fancy place."

"Not the Elite Lounge, I hope."

He laughed. "Connor would kill me. No, it's more exclusive than that dive."

She couldn't help herself. She had to touch him. Her hand seemed to rise of its own accord, and she laid her fingers against his cheek. Scratchy, in contrast to those liquid eyes and his thick, dark hair. He leaned into her touch, and her stomach lurched.

She backed up a step and almost sat down.

"Saturday," she got out. "Good night."

He was still standing there at the bottom of the stairs watching her when she reached the top and looked back. Well, now I've done it, Kate thought. I can't back out. Butterflies fluttered in her stomach. Neil raised one hand in a wave and turned away.

Neil lay looking up at the ceiling, watching the flickering light of the fire. He couldn't remember ever sleeping in the same room with a fireplace going. It made him think of the stories he used to read about knights and warriors. He wished this were his castle hall, and he could be the knight in shining—okay, tarnished—armor for…

Kate.

He hadn't planned on letting her—or any woman—turn his life upside down again. He'd determined six months earlier to put his social life on hold and learn what God expected of him. If that included love and marriage, he wanted to go by the book—God's book.

And here was Kate, and he wasn't ready. Or was he?

He pulled the small Bible that Connor and Adrienne had given him for Christmas from his duffel bag and switched on his flashlight. He read through II Corinthians 5, not sure he understood it all, but phrases here and there jumped out at him. "So we make it our goal to please Him." He read that verse several times, then put the book and flashlight aside. He lay back on his pillow and prayed that he would not fail in his goal.

He woke up hours later. His senses reeled as he became aware that he wasn't in his own bed. Wood smoke. He opened his eyes. The lights were back on in Connor's living room. The fire had died down, but the furnace was humming. He looked at his watch. Twenty minutes past four. He sat up, pulled his jeans on and went around turning off lights. The study, the entry, the kitchen. The sunroom and the bedroom were dark.

He tiptoed back to the living room and shut off the overhead light. The DVD player flashed 12:00 in red. He crawled back into bed and rolled over, turning away from the annoying strobe.

At six-thirty he woke again to the smell of coffee. He jumped out of bed and grabbed his duffel. Adrienne was in the kitchen, fixing breakfast.

"Good morning, Neil. We've got power!"

"Yeah. That's great. Can I take a shower?"

"Absolutely."

When he emerged from the bathroom fifteen minutes later, Connor was eating scrambled eggs and toast. Adrienne had set a place for Neil with a glass of orange juice and a cup of coffee. He sat down and prayed silently. It was good to have hot food.

Connor said, "Let's hope Augusta's got power, too. We've got so much to do today."

Kate entered the kitchen carrying Matthew. They both looked rumpled and still a little sleepy. Neil jumped up to pull out a chair for her, and couldn't help thinking how beautiful she was.

Matthew fussed a little and dove from her lap into his father's arms.

"Good morning, buddy." Connor kissed him and tickled him.

"Sleep all right?" Kate asked.

Neil nodded. "I dreamed I was in a medieval castle, sleeping in the great hall. All of a sudden, a fire was blazing all around me. I woke up and realized the electricity was back on."

He called his mother before they left the house. The Alexanders were still in darkness. "It shouldn't be long," he told her. "Connor and Adrienne have power."

"Ask if they need anything," said Connor.

His mother assured him they were coping. Adrienne started calling their friends to see if anyone who was still without power needed to take showers or do laundry. The streets were still icy, but the city crews had sanded them during the night. Neil watched Kate drive out cautiously, heading for the newspaper office. He followed Connor to the police station on Middle Street.

It was Neil's job to call every airline that flew into Portland and ask if they had a reservation for Joseph Parlin any time between Christmas Eve and January twentieth.

On the second try, he hit pay dirt.

"Connor," he called across the office, "Parlin had—or I should say, has—a reservation for January fifteenth. Flying to New York, then on to Paris."

"When did he book the flight?" Connor asked.

"December tenth. And even though he's changed his timetable, he didn't cancel the reservation."

"He didn't make another one?"

"They've looked and didn't find anything. The other airlines haven't, either."

"Maybe he decided to drive to Boston or New York and fly from there," Tony said.

"Possibly," Connor conceded.

"Well, you don't think he's still planning to fly out of Portland on the fifteenth?" Neil asked.

"He probably just abandoned the reservation. But still…"

Neil grinned at him. "There's something else. Mr. *and Mrs.* Parlin have reservations."

"First name for the Mrs.?" Connor asked.

"Letter *R*."

"Thought they required a full name now."

"Apparently this one got by them."

Connor rubbed the back of his neck. "I *knew* there was a woman in on it." He called Mike, and the chief came downstairs to pray. Tony and Lance made themselves scarce, but Jimmy joined them.

They prayed earnestly about the case. Afterward, they talked about it some more. Neil told Mike about the plane reservation for Mr. and Mrs. Parlin.

"He wouldn't use that reservation," Mike said.

Connor agreed. "He knows we're onto him now."

"But he doesn't know we're onto the Parlin identity," Neil said.

Connor frowned. "I would surely like to know who Mrs. Parlin is."

"Suppose it's Mrs. Burton," said Jimmy.

"No way," Neil said.

Connor shook his head. "She'd be leaving Stephen and Sean behind. I can't see her doing that."

"She got pretty plastered the day we searched the house," Neil mused.

"Think she's an alcoholic?" asked Mike.

"Maybe," said Neil. "But she came to bail her son out the next morning. She was sober then."

"I was just thinking about why Burton would leave her and the boys," said Connor.

"All right," said Mike. "*Cherchez la femme.* This Natalie DeWitt is probably not the one. But someone is. Check out every woman in his life. Whoever 'Mrs. Parlin' is, she's out there somewhere."

"I suspect she's long gone," said Connor. "She picked him up at the restaurant, and they drove off into the sunset."

"You don't suppose they'd lie low until the fifteenth, then show up at Kennedy and try to use the reservation to Paris?" Neil asked.

"Alert the airline people," Connor said. "They'd have to have passports under the assumed names. I'll check that now."

He phoned the State Department, and Neil called the airline and asked them to keep an eye on the Parlin reservation and alert the Portland police immediately if it was canceled or if another reservation was made in that name.

Connor was on hold. He hated to be on hold. Neil poured him a cup of coffee and put it at his elbow. "Thanks," the captain murmured. "Check missing persons, would you?"

On the computer, Neil checked the complaint records since the day Jim Burton had disappeared. One teenager had been reported missing. A man was missing during the ice storm, but had been found keeping warm at a friend's house. That was all, other than Burton. People stayed close to home in winter.

Connor came over to his desk. "Got it," he said. "Joseph Parlin applied for a passport in August. They'll send me a copy."

"How about the Mrs.?"

"They're not sure, since I didn't have the first name. They're searching for any female by the last name Parlin who applied since August first."

"What now?"

"I'm going to call the French embassy and see if they applied for visas. They might have, if they plan to stay there long."

"Did you get an address from the State Department, where they mailed his passport?" Neil asked.

"A P.O. box. Why don't you and Tony go to the post office

and check it out? Take the Burton and Parlin pictures. See if he's still using the box."

"And if he is?"

"We'll get a warrant and check his mail."

ELEVEN

At the post office, the postmaster took Tony and Neil back to the sorting area. Neil explained to him that the patron had rented the box under an assumed name. He showed him a photo of James Burton and the driver's license photo of his alter ego, Joseph Parlin. The postmaster checked the record of the rental and gave him the street address the renter had given. It was the empty house in Westbrook.

The postmaster checked the box. There were several flyers and a piece of first-class mail in the box.

"I can't give it to you," he told Neil.

"We'll come back with a warrant." Neil handed him his business card.

"Call me immediately if anyone picks up the mail from Parlin's box."

"Should we stake out the post office?" Tony asked Connor when they returned to the police station. "The clerks might not notice when the mail is picked up."

"Highly unlikely he's hanging around and picking up his mail," said Connor.

"Someone might pick it up for him," Neil said.

Connor called the courthouse, then sent Tony for the warrant. "I'm still waiting to hear from the State Department," he told Neil. When Tony came back, he still had no word, and it was lunchtime. The three of them went to the diner down the street. The inside of the restaurant was small and dim and made Neil claustrophobic, but it was close to the station and cheap, and the food was pretty good. He asked the blessing aloud, and Tony was tolerant enough to ignore it without looking terribly embarrassed. The guys seemed to be getting used to Connor's and Neil's penchant for prayer.

The warrant had arrived when they returned, and Neil went back to the post office and retrieved Parlin's mail. The first-class item was a six-month visa confirmation for Joseph and Doreen Parlin.

"Doreen?" asked Connor, when Neil took it to him. "Any Doreens in his life?"

"Not that I know of," Neil said. "Another assumed name. I was hoping she'd use her real first name."

"We're missing something," Connor insisted. "This woman had to build a false identity, just like Burton did."

Tony said, "Do you think they went so far as to get a fake marriage license?"

"No," said Connor, "but she'd need a driver's license, or at least a birth certificate and Social Security number, or she'd never get a passport."

"Do you know that she has a passport?" Neil asked.

"She must. They got the visa confirmation and booked the plane tickets to Paris."

"So what do we do?"

"*Cherchez la femme*, like Mike said. There's a woman who's close to him. We've got to find her. I'll check the DMV for women named Parlin who've applied for a driver's license. You two get a list of every woman Burton associated with through the shelter. Ask Mrs. Burton about friends, neighbors, anyone they socialized with."

"That sort of backfired the last time," Neil reminded him.

"Maybe not. I've put in a request for an undercover unit to tail Natalie DeWitt tonight. Meanwhile, let's scrutinize the other women he knew."

Neil said, "Okay, but do me a favor. Send someone else to Mrs. Burton this time. I think she hates me."

Lance and Jimmy got that assignment. Tony and Neil went

to the animal shelter. Roberta Palmer gave them a list of all the employees and another of volunteers.

"Is this complete?" Neil asked. "Are there any others who used to work here or volunteer here, but have quit in the past six months?"

"You're asking for a lot," she said, but she went to work on it. Tony started questioning the women who were working in the office that day, and Neil talked to the ones working in the kennel.

"The vet is here today," said Amelia Weston, who was in charge of the kennels during the workday. "We're really busy."

Neil tried not to get in the way. As she carried puppies to the veterinarian for their vaccinations, he questioned her about her relationship with Burton and watched her closely. Her calm demeanor convinced him she'd never heard the name Joseph Parlin before. He asked her if she thought it was possible Jim Burton had a girlfriend.

"After what he did, I'd say anything's possible," she replied. "He knows how badly we need a new facility."

"Do you think he might have had a liaison with someone who worked here?"

"Can't think who, unless it was one of the volunteers. None of the regular staff has a mystery man in her life that I know of."

"How about the volunteers?" Neil asked, holding out the list to her.

"Well, the college students come in on Monday," Amelia said.

"College students?"

"Yes, these three girls."

"Think one of them might have cozied up to the boss?"

"I wouldn't have thought so, but really, who can say? I don't think anything could shock me worse than Jim walking off with that money."

Neil called the dean's office at the university, but classes wouldn't resume until the next Monday. Most of the students were away from campus for vacation.

Connor had no word from the State Department when they returned to the office, but he had found three women named Parlin who had obtained new Maine driver's licenses since July. He showed the photos to his men. One was a sixty-year-old, gray-haired woman who had moved to Maine from New York.

"I think we can rule her out," Tony said. "Burton was rubbing elbows with coeds at the shelter."

"Okay, look at this next picture," said Connor. "This girl just got her license for the first time. We are really hoping it's not her, because she's only seventeen."

Tony and Neil shook their heads. "There are a couple of high school girls on the list of volunteers at the shelter, but we haven't seen them yet," Neil said.

"Okay, this one had a Maine license and moved out of state for a while, then came back in October. What do you think?"

She was forty-one. Her hair was pulled back, and she wore glasses with chunky, dark frames. Hard to say whether she was pretty or not.

"Never seen her," said Tony.

"I don't know," Neil said cautiously. "Can you take the dorky glasses off her and give her a different hairstyle?"

"I'll try with the computer. If that doesn't work for you, maybe the sketch artist can."

"What's her name?" Neil asked.

"Rena Parlin. Address in Gorham," Connor said.

"Rena. That's awfully close to Doreen."

"That's what I thought. And the plane ticket said 'R. Parlin.' She's our best bet so far."

Neil set about calling women on the lists of shelter workers and volunteers. He felt as if they were moving backward in the investigation, although Tony did tentatively rule out the two high school volunteers.

Late in the afternoon, Connor got a fax from the State Department. It was a copy of Doreen Parlin's passport application, and included a dark, smeary copy of a tiny photo.

"That's awful," Neil said. "Can't tell a thing."

Connor called them again. His contact had left for the day.

"Go home and get a dose of Adrienne and those beautiful kids," Neil told him.

"I will," Connor said. "I just keep seeing Jim Burton and his girlfriend driving along in a convertible, laughing and getting farther and farther away."

Connor's calls to the State Department finally paid off the next day. A copy of Doreen Parlin's passport photo came in electronically at 11:30 a.m. Same glasses as the Rena Parlin driver's license. Her hair was short.

"She cut her hair," said Tony.

Lance scowled at the photo. "Could be a wig."

"Rena/Doreen," Neil said, comparing the two pictures. "Definitely the same woman."

"The question is, where have we seen her before?" Connor brought up the program they used to build sketches of suspects and keyed in the face shape, eyes, nose, mouth and eyebrows. No glasses. Then he tried to fill in the gaps. He showed the results to his men. The same woman with a short, curly perm; with long, straight hair; and with a bouncy flip.

"No use," said Tony.

"I think I have seen her," Neil said.

Connor sat with his chin on his hands, staring at the screen.

"Can we take lunch?" Tony asked.

"Sure." He didn't look up.

"You going to eat?" Neil asked.

"I'm taking my lunch hour late, to meet Adrienne at the pediatrician's office."

"I'll bring you something," Neil offered.

"I'm okay." Connor still stared at the monitor.

Neil and Tony went to the diner. Neil ate hurriedly and ordered a BLT and milk for Connor.

"What's the rush?" Tony asked.

"Connor's in overdrive. Take your time. I just need to get back there."

He picked up the bag, paid for the food and walked quickly back to the station. Connor met him on the stairs.

"Neil! Come on!"

"Where?"

"The animal shelter."

Neil turned around and went with him to the garage. "I'll drive, you eat." He handed Connor the bag and unlocked his truck. "Who are we after?" he asked, turning onto Franklin Street from the parking lot.

"Roberta Palmer."

"No way."

"Yes. It's her."

"Can't be."

"It is. I don't know how she did it, but she did. The glasses and makeup and a wig, I guess. Maybe caps on her front teeth."

"But Burton left over a week ago," Neil protested.

"And now who is in charge of the huge fund-raiser? Who is giving the orders at the shelter and collecting the money from advance sales on tickets and putting it in the bank every afternoon?"

"Roberta Palmer. I still don't believe it. She helped us."

"Sure she did. As long as we believe she had a businesslike relationship with Burton and was shocked when he left with the money, she'll help you investigate anyone *else* connected with the shelter."

"All right, eat."

"Not hungry."

"Call Adrienne, at least. You're going to miss her appointment."

"Oh, man, I can't do that. It's Hailey's first checkup." Connor looked at his watch. "If we're quick, I can still make it to the doctor's."

"We'd better call for backup to take Ms. Palmer in," Neil said.

"Let's make sure she's there first. She may be out to lunch."

When Neil had parked at the shelter, Connor held out the driver's license and passport photos to him.

Neil looked closely at the pictures, and began to see it. "Okay, it's her. But the nose isn't right somehow."

"It's the glasses. Makes her nose look thinner. Maybe her makeup contributes to that, too. But it's her. Come on."

They went in, and a woman who was typing looked up. "Detective Alexander. May I help you?"

"I'd like to speak to Miss Palmer."

"Roberta left for the day."

"Did she say why?" Neil asked.

"She wasn't feeling well."

"When did she leave?"

"About half an hour ago."

"And her home address is…?"

"Is it urgent?"

"Yes," Neil said, feeling Connor's energy beside him.

Connor walked to Roberta's desk, picked up a phone book and opened it.

"We need to see her right away," Neil said.

"Well, I… She lives in Woodfords."

Connor snapped an address out, reading it from the phone book.

"Yes," said the typist, "that's it."

Connor was out the door, and Neil followed.

"I'm dropping you at the doctor's office," Neil said. "It's not that far."

"We'll lose her."

"No. She doesn't know we're onto her."

"Then why did she leave work early?"

"Maybe she's really sick," Neil said.

"Right." Connor's sarcasm made him wince.

"I'll call Tony and have him meet me."

"Go to Woodfords."

"You can't stand Adrienne up," Neil insisted.

Connor pulled his cell phone out and punched two buttons. He smiled when she answered. "Hey, gorgeous. Afraid I'm not going to make it this time. I know. I'm sorry."

"I can have you there in three minutes," Neil said.

"Go—to—Woodfords," Connor ground out. Neil got the message.

Ten minutes later, they pulled in at a green duplex with peeling paint. The driveway on Roberta's side was empty, and no one came to the door.

Connor went to the other side, and a woman holding a baby opened the door. He showed his badge.

"I'm looking for Roberta Palmer."

"She works at the animal shelter," the woman said.

"Yes, but she's not there today. Have you seen her?"

"Not since she left this morning."

They got back in the truck, and Neil steered a course straight for the doctor's office without saying anything.

"The bank," said Connor.

"Huh?"

"The bank where they put the ticket money. She's withdrawing it as we speak."

Neil hit the brakes. "What bank did they use?"

"It's the same one Burton lifted the building fund from." Connor closed his eyes and gritted his teeth. "Central Bank. Yeah, that's it. Let's put the light on." Connor reached to the dashboard and turned on the blue light. Neil drove to the bank. They left the truck at the curb in a no-parking spot, strobe light still going.

Neil looked all around as they went in. "She's not here, Connor."

"That means we're too late." Connor bypassed the lines and said to a teller, "I'm Captain Larson with the Portland P.D. I need to see the manager immediately."

She waved him toward the opposite end of the building, and

Connor turned and strode along a line of small private offices with glass walls. The last one was larger than the others. The manager was talking with a client. Connor knocked and opened the door.

"Sir, I'm Captain Larson with the Portland P.D. I'm sorry to interrupt you, but we've got an emergency here."

Donald Sharpe came quickly out of the office, excusing himself to the client.

"The Animal Protection Society may have been robbed again," Connor said. "They have their account here still?"

"Yes. We've been very careful about security since the embezzlement."

"Really? Would you just check for me and see if the account has had any activity today?"

Sharpe looked at him keenly, then went to a vacant teller's station and began tapping at the computer keyboard.

Sharpe's face turned red. He called a teller to him and brought her out to where the detectives waited.

"Follow me," he said, and led them down a set of stairs and into a conference room. He turned and faced the teller. "Mrs. Jordan, the Animal Protection Society's savings account was emptied a few minutes ago. You gave them cash."

"Minutes?" said Connor. "Minutes?"

"At twelve twenty-three," said Sharpe.

Neil and Connor both looked at their watches.

"Back to Woodfords, Neil." Connor was out the door and up the stairs.

Neil followed, leaving the poor teller alone to face Sharpe's wrath. He heard her say, "Mrs. Palmer came in and said they—"

"She won't be there," Neil said to Connor as they got in the truck.

"Where will she be?"

"Heading for Burton."

Connor pulled out the radio handpiece and called the dispatcher. "APB on Roberta Palmer, alias Rena or Doreen Parlin. Check the DMV info on her vehicle." Next he called Tony on his cell phone. "Tony, get on the computer. If Lance and Jimmy are there, have them help you. We need information on any and all vehicles registered to Roberta Palmer from the animal shelter, and also the fictional Joseph and Doreen or Rena Parlin." He rattled off Roberta Palmer's address. "Got it?"

Apparently Wonder Boy got it, because Connor put the phone away and sat fuming. Neil could almost see smoke coming out his ears.

"Don't beat yourself up, Connor."

His friend pounded the armrest with his fist. "Why didn't I recognize her immediately?"

"Because it was a good disguise. I've been over there three or four times now, and I couldn't see it."

Connor sighed and ran his hand through his hair.

When they got to the duplex, there was still no car in Roberta's driveway. They pounded on the door, but got no response. The neighbor in the other side of the house opened her door.

"You looking for Roberta again?"

"Yes!" Connor cried.

"She was here just a minute ago. I told her you were here. She ran in the house for a minute and came right back out and left. Had a suitcase."

"Was anyone else in the car?"

"I didn't see anyone."

They raced back to the truck. "Now where?" Neil asked.

Connor looked utterly lost. "Airport, I guess." He took out his phone again and called the chief, filling Mike in as Neil drove with the blue light flashing.

"They've got a description of Roberta's car. Mike's going to put roadblocks out right away," he told Neil. "But if she stays off the interstate, there's not a lot of hope."

It took Neil almost fifteen minutes to get to the airport. He parked in the unloading zone. Connor jumped out and ran inside. Neil called the dispatcher with their location and asked for as many units as the department could send. Then he got out, locked the truck and followed.

Inside the terminal, he looked around for Connor. When he looked up, he saw the captain disappear into the airport manager's office on the upper level. Neil quickly scanned the ticket lines and waiting areas on the lower level, then went up the escalator. He cased the café area, then the newsstand, looking for Roberta Palmer. When he came out of the newsstand, Connor and the manager were approaching with a uniformed officer.

"Three units on the way," Neil said.

"Good," said Connor. "Put two of them on the garage and parking areas to look for her car." The manager went through a metal detector, into the passengers-only area.

"He's going to hold every plane until it's searched. Nothing takes off until we search it. Airport security will help, and we'll close the entry doors until we know if she's here. Let me know immediately if you find her car." Connor went through the gate after the manager, showing his badge.

Neil hurried downstairs and out to the driveway. Two units were pulling up. He gave the four officers the license plate number and description of the vehicle, and they headed for the parking garage. Neil went to the exit gate, where people leaving the airport paid for their parking time, and asked the attendant if he'd seen the car. He didn't think he had. Neil impressed on him that he needed to watch carefully for it and call the manager on his cell phone immediately if he saw it.

Back at the front of the terminal, security guards were at the doors, telling irate passengers they would have to wait, and assuring them that their planes would not leave without them. A third squad car came in with shrieking siren. Neil put the patrol officers in the outside parking areas, looking for Roberta's car. He scanned the burgeoning crowd on the sidewalk.

Patrolman Ray Oliver came running from the parking garage. "Her car's on the second level. It's locked up. What do you want us to do?"

"Just watch it for now," Neil said. He called Connor on his cell phone.

"Her car's in the garage, Connor. You were right."

"Okay, we're about to board a plane that's holding for takeoff. Show the ticket agents at U.S. Air the pictures and see if they recognize her."

Neil went inside and approached the airline counter. When the agent shook her head over the photos, Neil described Roberta without the disguise—forty, red hair, attractive. His cell phone rang. Connor.

"Tell security to open the doors, and meet me in the manager's office. We've got her!"

TWELVE

Neil relayed the message, then went up to the airport manager's office on the mezzanine. Roberta was mad. Very mad. She sat in a steel and vinyl chair with her hands cuffed in front of her. She wore a dark, short wig and the unflattering glasses.

"Where is it?" Connor was asking her.

She looked balefully at him, but said nothing.

"Let's go," he said. They took her down a service elevator and out to one of the squad cars.

Ray Oliver stepped up and said to Connor, "Do you want us to tow the car, sir?"

Connor gave instructions and dismissed the other units. They took Roberta back to the station, and Connor assigned Tony to book her.

While Neil waited, Connor paced from the window, past his desk, to the corner of Neil's and back.

"She dropped the money somewhere," he said. "They pulled her luggage off the plane, and it wasn't there."

"Maybe she checked another bag," Neil suggested.

"No, they looked into that. I left them tearing that airplane apart. The passengers are probably still on the runway, furious at us."

"She went home after she left the bank," Neil reminded him.

Connor called Ron Legere and asked for a search team to go immediately to Roberta Palmer's house. "Make sure they ask the neighbor if anyone else has been there besides me," he told Ron. When he had hung up, he sighed, scratching his head. "Why did she pick today?"

"Yesterday was the last day for the advance tickets for the ball," Neil said. "All the money was in by five o'clock yesterday."

"Guess we should have thought of that."

"That's what they were waiting for. But where was she headed?"

"JFK," Connor said. "Then who knows where? She didn't have a connecting flight booked."

"Maybe she was going to stay in New York a week, then use the reservation on the Paris flight."

"Or maybe…" Connor stopped by the window.

"What are you thinking?" Neil asked.

"A third ID. She'd booked this ticket under the name Roberta Jones. She had another phony driver's license that got her past security and onto the plane. Maybe she's got a passport under that name, too. Still, if she does, she didn't have it with her."

"It's really hard to get one bogus passport, let alone two," Neil said.

"Maybe she had to get it quickly and bought a phony one instead of applying for a legitimate one this time. Forgers make passports."

"They usually don't get by customs," Neil replied.

"Have we still got Patrick in the lockup?"

Neil called downstairs. "He went to the county jail."

Mike came into the room from the stairway. "You got her. Good work."

"Pulled her out of the bathroom on a plane they stopped on the runway. One more minute…" Connor shook his head. "She stashed the money somewhere. I honestly don't think she took it on the plane."

"She could have asked someone else to carry it," said Mike.

"They warn people about that now," said Connor. "But they'll question all the other passengers anyway."

"Well, they don't have lockers at the airport," Neil said. "It's got to be somewhere."

"The real question is, where's Burton?" Mike said.

Connor shrugged. "He wasn't on that plane."

"She was going to meet him somewhere," said Mike.

"She was flying to New York," Neil told him. "Maybe he was picking her up there."

Mike nodded. "Call JFK. Send the photos of Burton with and without his disguise. Ask them to check all the people meeting that plane."

Neil went to his desk and began the process of trying to get through to the right people in time. He sent the photos as e-mail attachments. He heard Connor telling Lance and Jimmy to go to the county jail and take copies of Roberta's forged documents to show Patrick. "If he didn't make them, ask him who did. He might recognize the work of another artist. And we want to know if she had anything else made."

Connor said to Mike, "If Burton was meeting her, he could have been holding more documents for her. Like a passport with the name Jones."

The chief of security at the JFK terminal came on the line, and Neil told him what was needed. He promised quick action.

Neil swiveled his chair so that his back was to Connor's desk and put a quick call through to Kate's cell phone. The pleasure in her voice when she greeted him sent his pulse galloping and made him realize how badly he wanted their relationship to work. "Kate, big news. We're holding a press conference at four-thirty. Can you come?"

"Absolutely. But can't you give me a little hint what it's about?"

He smiled. She always pressed her advantage. Well, he could do that, too. "Sure, but first tell me we're still on for tomorrow."

"What's tomorrow?"

"You know. My Oma. I set it up with her for tomorrow afternoon. She can't wait to meet you."

"Excellent! I can't wait to meet her, either."

Neil grinned. "And…I was thinking…dinner afterward? And the show at the Civic Center?"

"You mean…"

"They've got the Lipizzaner stallions this weekend."

"I know, I know. Barry did a story about them. But the tickets are exorbitant."

"Is it a deal?"

"Yes, of course. But you don't have to spend all that money."

"Hush. Just make sure you get to the press conference on time. We arrested Roberta Palmer about an hour ago."

"Roberta Palmer? That nice woman at the animal shelter?"

"Uh-huh. Up to her neck in this with Jim Burton."

She exhaled audibly. "Wow."

The elevator doors opened, and Tony got off with Roberta.

"I've got to go," Neil said.

He and Connor took the prisoner into the interrogation room. Mike stuck around, and Neil figured he'd be in Observation with Tony.

"All right, Roberta," said Connor, when the tape was rolling, "do you want to tell me about it?"

"No."

"You'll wish you had."

"I'd rather wait until I see my lawyer."

"Did you ask for a lawyer downstairs?"

"Yes."

"Then he's probably on his way. Miss Palmer, I don't understand your thinking in this whole business."

"So formal now, Captain?"

Connor bowed his head slightly.

"You thought he'd never be interested in me," she said. "It never even occurred to you. You thought he was after one of those college girls." She laughed bitterly.

"Whose idea was this, anyway?" Connor asked. "You thought it out months in advance, laid your plans together."

"I suppose we both did. We just thought of it one night. It was simple, getting hold of the money. It was stacking up fast, and we made sure at least half of it stayed in accounts we could access quickly. Jim had the authority to manage the accounts. Later, when he left, I managed them."

"But you planned to go the fifteenth, after the Fur Ball," said Connor.

"That was a bit of a miscalculation," she said. "We should have planned it earlier. When I realized all of the receipts would be in a week early, it was a bit of a letdown. We'd have to stick around the extra week, acting innocent."

Neil stood under the video camera, at the side of the room nearest the door, watching her. She was attractive, now that she had shed the wig and glasses.

"We have your false documents, under the name Parlin," Connor said. "We know Burton assumed the identity of his dead cousin. You would never have been able to leave the country."

She said nothing.

"So Jim found himself in a spot, and he had to leave early. He was looking at two murder charges. You, of course, will be charged as an accessory. You were probably the one who heard Ted Hepburn talking to Edna Riley about his apprehension. Something wasn't right at the shelter, and Ted knew it. You told Jim." Connor waited.

"I told you, I'd like to speak to my attorney," Roberta said.

Connor said to Neil, "Take her downstairs." To her, he added, "We'll talk again later."

When Neil returned to the office, Connor was hunched before his computer again. Neil shoved his hands in his pockets and walked over to the captain's corner desk.

"What do we do now?"

Connor grinned without looking away from his screen. "Hang in there, buddy. It's almost time for the press conference. Go ahead down there. I think I've found the bank where the shelter's money ended up. If we can get authority to freeze that account and keep Burton from accessing it…"

Neil eyed him thoughtfully. "You'll be taking his million away from him. Then he'll be desperate."

"He sure will. And that's when he's most likely to make a mistake."

The tall young man seated himself across from Kate in a booth at the fast food restaurant down the street from the pizza place.

"Thanks for agreeing to see me on short notice, Stephen."

He shrugged, not quite meeting her gaze. "Well, it's better than where I work. I wouldn't want my boss hearing me talk about this."

"I understand."

Stephen Burton brushed the hair out of his eyes. "I'm not sure why you want to talk to me. I mean…if you put something more in the paper about me, my mother would probably die. First she'd kill me, then she'd die."

Kate smiled and cocked her head to one side. "It's not my intention to embarrass your family. I know this last week has been very difficult for you."

"Yeah. Especially Mom. When she told me and Sean that Dad was gone, it was…" He glanced up for a moment. "She was miserable. Please don't make her feel that way again."

"What did she say when your father took off?" Kate asked.

"She said at first that he probably had to leave on business in a hurry and would call us that day. But he didn't. She started making calls to see if he'd checked in at his office or the shelter, but he hadn't. So finally she reported him missing. She hated to. I guess we all wanted to believe he'd walk in the door any minute."

"And when the detectives found that his gun had been used in a couple of murders?"

He drew a quick breath and looked out the window. "She said it was a mistake, and he wouldn't kill anyone."

"The police have asked the newspaper not to publicize the fact that the murder weapon belonged to your father, even though we know it."

He eyed her cautiously, his brows drawn together in a frown. "Why would you hold something back like that? I mean, could they arrest you if you published it? I thought reporters were all for exposure and getting the truth out, no matter who it hurt."

Kate felt her color rising. It stung to know people thought that, and she felt a modicum of shame on behalf of all journalists, because there was probably some truth to what he said.

"To be honest, I agreed not to publish it because I want to help the police if I can. They think holding back certain information may help them catch the killer. I'm not saying that was your father, Stephen. Someone else could have used his gun to do that."

"Someone else did, if his gun really was the murder weapon. I'm not convinced that's true."

"You think the police are wrong about that? Because the tests they use to match bullets to the weapons that fired them are highly accurate."

"Yeah? Well, maybe they lied about it."

Kate frowned. "Why would the detectives do that?"

"To scare us into spilling something. To make us say something incriminating about my father."

She swallowed hard. "Stephen, I can assure you that those men wouldn't do that. I know Detective Alexander and Captain Larson personally, and they wouldn't lie to anyone to try to trick them. They have to ask painful questions sometimes. That's part of their job. But if they told you those people were killed with your father's handgun, then it's true."

He scowled. "Whatever. Anyway, I was stupid to take the gun, and to shoot at that cat. But I went to court, and it's over. That has nothing to do with my father. I don't know what's going on with him. You make it sound like he's out there reading the paper, and you're being careful not to tell him what the cops know about the gun. Why?"

Kate hesitated. Had she made a huge blunder in asking Stephen for an interview? Maybe she should have asked Connor's opinion first.

"You think Dad killed those people," Stephen said.

"The ballistics tests are foolproof. It was the same gun." She fished her small notebook from her purse and flipped through it to the notes she'd made when she'd talked to Neil about Stephen's interrogation at the police station. "You told the detectives that you saw your father holding it last Tuesday night. Cleaning it. And someone had used it just a few days before to shoot two old people."

He coldly met her stare. "Not my dad."

"But if someone stole it and used it to commit the murders, how did your dad get it back in time to clean it Tuesday evening?"

"I don't know." Stephen turned angrily to one side, sweeping his forearm across the tabletop. Kate grabbed her coffee cup and set it over against the wall. "Look, Dad and I weren't all that buddy-buddy the last couple of years. He didn't tell me everything."

Kate waited a moment, until his breathing settled down a little. Gently, she said, "You took it from his closet Thursday morning, and he disappeared that day. I'm asking you, can you really believe he had nothing to do with it?"

"Somebody set him up."

"Aw, come on, Stephen." She kept her voice low, hoping not to attract attention. It was three-thirty in the afternoon, and only a sprinkling of diners occupied the other tables.

"Dad would not do that," Stephen insisted. "He's not the easiest person to get along with, but he's not a killer."

"How do you know?"

"I just know." Stephen's eyes were dark.

"That's not good enough. I'm telling you, the evidence says your father is a murderer." She leaned forward and held his gaze. So far, she wasn't getting much that she could print.

He surprised her by taking the initiative. "You obviously think you know what happened, so tell me what did. You think Dad wigged out and went on a rampage and started shooting old people he knew from the shelter?"

Kate shook her head. "No. I think it was very calculated and deliberate. Someone at the shelter heard Ted Hepburn and Edna Riley talking about how your father was going to steal the money and run off with it, and that person told your father, and he went and killed them both."

Stephen's jaw dropped. "He wouldn't…"

"Yes, he did." She let that sink in, then looked at her watch. "When I leave here, do you know where I'm going?"

He shook his head.

"I'm going over to the police station. They've arrested Miss Palmer. Do you know Roberta Palmer from the shelter?"

He nodded.

"My front-page story tomorrow will be all about how they arrested her this afternoon. They're holding a press conference in an hour. It will be on the Internet and the television news tonight. Miss Palmer helped your father steal the Animal Protection Society's money. She was going to meet him today, but the police caught her."

"He said he didn't do it." Stephen turned away from her, staring out the window.

Kate gathered her things. "I'm sorry, Stephen. This probably wasn't a good time to interview you. I should have let the police or your mother tell you about this." He didn't respond, and she sighed. "Before I knew about Miss Palmer, I had thought maybe I could interview you and your mother and let you both tell your side of the story. I was hoping it would help uncover the truth. But now… This was a bad idea." She stood up.

"Wait," Stephen said. "What are you going to write about?"

She shrugged. "Miss Palmer's arrest, for sure."

"What are you going to say about my dad?"

"I don't know yet. I'll have to see what the police tell me at the press conference." Talking to Burton's son was an error in judgment. That was plain to her now. She hoped he wouldn't try to make trouble for her. If he weren't a fugitive, Jim Burton would no doubt have called her boss and demanded that she be fired.

"I'm sorry I upset you. I'm…still kind of new at this. I meant it when I said I want to help find the killer. If it's not your father, then I'd like to find the person who really did it. And I don't want to make things any harder than they are for your family."

He didn't lift his head.

"Well, thanks." She managed a smile and went out to her car, feeling a little sick.

Big, fluffy flakes of snow were falling. She decided to do a sidebar on Roberta Palmer, recapping her years at the animal shelter. In the short time between talking to Stephen and the press conference, she could squeeze in a telephone call to Amelia Weston, the kennel manager, and ask her if she could e-mail a summary of Roberta's service at the shelter.

A short time later, Kate drove toward the police station. She anticipated seeing Neil and maybe getting invited up to the Priority Unit afterward. Her pulse accelerated, and she knew it wasn't from the prospect of picking up tips for her story. Neil had claimed a huge percentage of her thoughts lately.

"Who am I kidding?" she said aloud. "I can't think of anyone else I'd even consider spending the rest of my life with. Lord, if this isn't right, please show us both."

She drove onto Middle Street and realized she wouldn't be able to park within three blocks of the police station. Maybe the garage behind? She signaled for another turn and let her thoughts drift back to the handsome detective.

She pulled in at the parking garage and grabbed a ticket from the machine, then nosed into a parking spot on the ground floor. She jumped out of the car and locked the door, pocketing her keys. Gotta hurry! As she dashed for the police station, she couldn't help replaying the interview with Stephen in her mind.

All of a sudden, she caught her breath as some of the young man's last words echoed in her mind. *He said he didn't do it.*

THIRTEEN

As the other reporters asked questions of the police department's spokesman, Kate edged around toward the stairway door. Neil was leaning against the wall. He smiled in greeting and squeezed over to make room for her beside him.

"I need to talk to you when this is over," she whispered.

He nodded, and she tried to focus on the question-and-answer session, jotting notes on the saga of Roberta Palmer's arrest. Good thing she'd thought to call Amelia Weston before this got out. Every reporter in Portland would be pestering the shelter staff now.

When the conference was dismissed, Neil quirked his eyebrows. "Want to come upstairs?"

"Sure."

He punched in a numerical code on the keypad beside the heavy door and swung it open. "The stairs are always faster than the elevator."

They trudged up the steps together and into the Priority Unit office. It was nearly empty—only Paula, the secretary, and Lance Miller were at their desks.

Neil took Kate to his workstation and pulled over an extra chair. "So, what's up?"

"I talked to Stephen Burton this afternoon."

"You did? Why?"

Kate winced. "Looks like you think it was a bad idea. I was afraid of that."

"Well…I guess if you'd asked my opinion first, I'd have said to be careful and think out your questions ahead of time. I mean, he's not exactly squeaky clean, and his father's accused of a double homicide and grand theft."

She nodded soberly. "I did consider that. But you don't think Stephen is dangerous, do you?"

Neil shrugged. "The lady who owned the cat would think he is. Did you get anything interesting?"

"Kind of. Nothing I can print, you understand. I talked to him for ten or fifteen minutes and decided I'd made a mistake. I felt kind of sleazy trying to get him to talk about his father, under the circumstances."

"I can see that. I mean, it's our job, but you don't want to use Jim Burton's son to smear him in the paper before he's convicted in the courts."

"Yeah." She scrunched up her face and then relaxed. "I told you it was a mistake. You would have seen that from the beginning."

He chuckled. "So, what are you up to now?"

"I have to go back to the office and write up this whole Roberta Palmer thing, but first, Stephen said something I thought you should know about."

"I'm listening."

"I…" She hesitated, belatedly wondering if she'd misused Neil's confidence. "Well, you know how you told me on the phone that Roberta was arrested?"

"Yes."

"Well, I sort of told Stephen that."

Neil's eyes narrowed, but after a moment he lifted his hands in dismissal. "If it was a secret, I wouldn't have told you. I mean, hundreds of people already knew. The airport staff, the passengers, the people trying to get into the terminal…"

"That's a relief. But, anyway, I'm afraid I pushed Stephen a little. See, he kept insisting that his father wouldn't kill those people. I told him it was true, and that you had proof Jim Burton's gun was the murder weapon. He still didn't want to believe me, so I told him you had arrested Ms. Palmer, and that she was in cahoots with his father. I told him they'd planned this for a long time, but then one of them heard Edna Riley and Ted Hepburn talking about it, and the next thing we know, those two volunteers are dead. I mean, that's what must have happened, don't you think?"

"It's a very interesting theory. It could very well be true. According to Gerald Riley, Edna heard the rumor from Ted. Could be he'd overheard or seen something at the shelter that made him suspect Burton wasn't on the up-and-up."

"And if Roberta heard him tell Edna, and she told Jim..."

Neil nodded. "I can see that happening."

"Yeah, well, when I put it out there, Stephen got angry. And here's the thing—he told me, 'He said he didn't do it.'"

Neil puffed out his breath. "Those were his words?"

"Yes. It didn't hit me at the time, but afterward I realized that was tantamount to admitting he'd been in communication with his father."

"Should we pick Stephen up again?" Neil asked Connor ten minutes later.

Connor shook his head and stared at his computer screen. "I should have known Kate wouldn't leave this alone. Who knows how much she gave that kid?"

"Well, Burton would have heard it all on the six o'clock news anyway."

"Yeah, but..." Connor sighed and leaned back in his chair. "I was actually toying with the idea of giving her a tip, to see if she could help us flush Burton out. Let her put out the word that we've made it impossible for him to get at that million dollars." He looked up at Neil with a grimace. "I wanted to make him desperate enough to make a move."

"Desperate men do awful things, Connor."

His friend nodded. "I wanted him to show himself, and maybe lead us to that money from the fund-raiser that Roberta Palmer stashed."

"That's all he's got now," Neil said. "If he checks with that bank in Aruba and knows he can't touch the million, he'll want to cut his losses and make a break for it. He needs that money from the Fur Ball."

"Yeah, I hear you. All right, we'll bring Stephen in again."

Connor's phone rang, and he snatched the receiver. "Larson. Yes? We'll be right there."

He stood as he replaced the receiver and reached for his jacket. "That was the postmaster. They've got a package for Joseph Parlin. Let's go." On his way out the door, he turned and looked the length of the office. "Lance! I need you to pick up Stephen Burton. Try his house, or that pizza place where he works."

"Isn't the post office closed now?" Neil asked as Connor steered his Explorer toward the main post office branch on Forest Avenue.

"Yes, but they've been sorting what came in today. One of the clerks made out a slip to put in the Parlin box for a package, and he saw the alert on the box and told the postmaster."

"Will he let us have the box?"

Connor shrugged. "I should think so. That warrant we got yesterday ought to cover it."

The postmaster was waiting to unlock the door for them. "I thought you'd want to know about this immediately."

"You got that right," Connor said.

The postmaster led them to the window area and brought out a Priority Mail box. "This was mailed about one o'clock at the branch on Congress Street. It…isn't likely to be a bomb, is it?" His bushy white eyebrows contracted anxiously.

"I don't think so," Connor replied. "Would you rather I opened it in the parking lot?" He shook it, listening carefully.

"No, go ahead."

Connor set it on a desk. "You got a box cutter?" Carefully he sliced through the adhesive that held the end of the box shut. He opened the flaps, peered inside and smiled. "Oh, yeah."

"Don't tell me," Neil said. "It's the money."

Connor nodded with satisfaction. "Two hundred grand. She may have kept a little out for travel expenses." He placed the box in Neil's hands. "Guess Roberta's mother never taught her not to send cash through the mail."

"Now what?" Neil asked.

Connor looked at the postmaster. "When's the soonest they can pick this up?"

"The lobby opens at 7:00 a.m. tomorrow, but the window isn't open until 8:00."

Neil said, "And you put a ticket in the mailbox that says he has a package, right?"

The man nodded. "Yes. If the box is too big for the mailbox, they have to bring the card to the window and pick it up."

"All right," Connor said. "We'll have a detective here by 6:45 a.m. Can you put one of my men in a postal worker's uniform and let him stand in here and watch to see who comes to get the mail?"

"I...suppose we could do that," the postmaster said. "He'll have to stay out of the way. We work fast around here."

"I'll send you somebody who knows what to do," Connor assured the man. "If someone comes for the box, let the detective give it to him. We'll have some plainclothesmen outside to follow the person who picks it up."

The postmaster nodded. "All right, if you think it won't endanger anyone."

"We'll do our best to make sure that doesn't happen. Now, I'll take this to the station, photograph the bills and lock it up overnight. The undercover officer will bring it back in the morning."

"That's an awful lot of cash, Captain."

"Yes, it is. But if I hadn't opened the box, you wouldn't have known what was in it, would you?"

"No."

"And where would the package have stayed tonight?"

"Over there in that bin, with those others for the box holders."

Connor nodded. "I think it will be safer with me, no offense intended. And trust me, I can make it look like it was never opened."

On the drive back to the police station, Neil asked, "You won't be too hard on Kate tonight, will you?"

Connor sighed. "She's impetuous. I'm afraid that's going to get her in trouble one of these days. She could easily have blown our investigation today. Neil, be careful how much information you give her."

"I will. And I'm sorry if I've let my personal relationship with her cloud my judgment on that."

"Well…anything she told Stephen Burton today, his father would have learned within hours anyhow. She's pretty sharp, though. I've got to hand her that."

"Yeah," Neil said. "She figured out the motive for the murders before we did."

"Uh-huh." Connor glanced over at him. "You still like her a lot, don't you?"

"Well…yeah. Is that a problem? Tell me now if it is."

Connor shook his head. "You're both adults, and the objections I had last summer no longer apply."

"Yes, we're both believers now. I'm a little nervous about it, but I'm starting to think God may approve of this."

Connor's solemn expression slowly morphed into a smile. "Keep asking God along the way, and you won't go wrong."

Kate arrived at the Larson home shortly after six o'clock. She carried her laptop and purse inside and met Adrienne in the kitchen. "I'm sorry I'm so late, Adri. I had to go back to the office and do my story after the press conference."

"Don't worry about it," her sister said. "Connor called at five and said he'd be late, too. I don't expect him for at least another hour. I've fed Matthew already, but I thought I'd wait on you two."

"Aunt Kate!" Matthew pulled on the hem of her sweater.

"Hey, buddy!" She swung him up into her arms. "Where's your precious sister?"

"She's having a nap," Adrienne said.

"Want to play with your blocks until Daddy gets home? We can build a castle."

Adrienne laughed. "I think he'd rather build a police station. Oh, your old roommate, Madyson, called."

"Yeah?"

"She says you left some boxes in the apartment."

Kate sighed and set Matthew on his feet. "I almost forgot. I left one last load of things that I couldn't fit in my car last week. I guess I can go over after supper, but I'm tired. I was looking forward to a quiet evening."

"No, she said she and the other girl will be out tonight."

"Too bad. I'm supposed to meet Neil's grandmother tomorrow."

"She said someone else is moving into your old room, so they need you to get your things as soon as possible."

Kate jounced Matthew up and down. "I guess I can pick them up in the morning. I'll have to try to get up and get moving early." She bent down to look into Matthew's eyes. "I'm going upstairs to change. You get the blocks out, okay?"

"That's no problem," Adrienne said. "They haven't been picked up all day."

"Well, we'll pick them up after we build a really cool police station, won't we, Matt?"

Kate sat down to dinner with Connor and Adrienne just after seven.

"Did you manage to talk to Stephen Burton again?" she asked.

"No. I sent a couple of men to pick him up, but he wasn't at his house or his job."

"Sorry."

He shrugged. "I don't know if your interview with Stephen will have a bearing on this case or not."

"But it proves his father is still in the area."

"Not really. He could have called him."

Kate stared down at her plate. "I'm really sorry, Connor. I should have checked with you before I tried to talk to him."

"Well, he is one of our witnesses, Kate. And that whole cat shooting thing… I wish you'd be a little more cautious, that's all."

She swallowed hard and nodded. "You're right. So, did you make any progress since you made the arrest at the airport?"

He inhaled slowly. "I did, but you know what? I can't tell you everything. I hope you understand that."

She felt the blood flow to her cheeks. "Because of my talking to Stephen?"

"No. There are just things I can't tell people until the time is right. But I hope that maybe tomorrow something will break in this case."

"You mean…the murders? Or the embezzling?"

"Both. There is one thing I *can* tell you. I questioned Roberta Palmer again this afternoon, when her lawyer was there."

Adrienne looked up at her husband eagerly. "Did she tell you where that money is? You said she withdrew it from the bank yesterday and got rid of it before you arrested her at the airport."

Connor bit his upper lip and smiled at her. "No, sweetheart. She didn't tell me what she did with it."

"She doesn't deny taking it out of the bank, does she?" Kate dared to ask.

Connor smiled at her, too, and she relaxed a little. He wasn't mad at her. "Oh, she admits withdrawing the money. We've got the bank security tapes and the teller's testimony, after all. But she says she had a perfect right to do that, which, in a way, she did. But she won't say what happened to it."

Kate was sure he knew a lot more than he was saying. "Did you ask her about Burton?"

"She claimed he was meeting her in New York with new documents, and they would leave the country for an unspecified destination. He was taking care of that end of it. She'd told him we were onto his Parlin persona. She figured we'd realize she was his partner in crime soon. That's why she bolted as soon as the ticket money was in. She claimed she was going to meet him at a hotel in Manhattan. But I checked with the hotel, and Burton was never there under his name or Parlin's. If he stayed there, or if he made a reservation, he used a different name."

"What does that mean?" Kate asked.

"Either she's lying to me, or Burton wasn't playing it straight with her."

Adrienne grimaced. "They sound like they deserve each other."

On Saturday morning, Neil took a shift on surveillance outside the post office. He sat in an unmarked car and watched the side door. He knew that Jimmy Cook was around the corner, watching the front entrance. Detective Emily Rood was inside, wearing the USPS uniform jacket.

It was a slow morning. Neil had plenty of time to ponder his potential future with Kate. She may be impulsive, but she was a crackerjack reporter. That might not be so good, though. She loved her job so much, she might not want to settle down. Would she be willing to give up her job someday to stay home with a baby, as Adrienne had done? Because Neil couldn't picture his own son or daughter in day care. And he did want children. More and more, he felt the urge to establish his own home and family.

I guess it's okay to pray about things like this, Lord. That woman in the Bible, Hannah, prayed for a baby. And I would like to be a father someday, if You'll let me. Show me if Kate is the right woman for me.

Fifteen minutes before the post office was due to close for the weekend, he spotted a familiar figure on the sidewalk. He radioed the other detectives on surveillance and then opened his cell phone and punched in Connor's home number.

"Connor, I just saw Sean Burton go into the post office."

"Did you say Sean? Not Stephen?"

"That's affirmative. Emily won't give him the package."

"She'd better not. His name's not on the paperwork for the post office box."

"Hang on. I'll tell you when he comes out."

"Neil, tail him. If he doesn't go home, I want to know where he goes. I can't believe Jim Burton's in touch with both boys."

"Maybe he's reconciled with his entire family, now that Roberta Palmer's out of the picture."

Less than five minutes later, Sean emerged from the building, his shoulders slumped. He hurried along the sidewalk, and Neil started his car. It soon became obvious that the boy was headed home.

"Get backup and check the house," Connor said. "I hate to do it, but I guess we've got to. If Jim Burton is back with his wife and is using his own home for headquarters…"

"You don't think he and Claire planned this all along, and he was just using Roberta to help get the money?" Neil asked.

"No. Well… Honestly? I have no idea."

FOURTEEN

Neil arrived early for their date, and Kate wasn't ready. He explained with a sheepish—but adorable—smile.

"I came early on purpose so I could brief Connor before we go see Oma."

"Oh," Kate said. "Well, I guess I'd better leave you two alone, then."

Neither of them contradicted her or invited her to sit in on the session, so she jogged up the stairs, trying not to let it bother her. She couldn't help wondering if Connor regretted being so open with her at the beginning. He had definitely narrowed the information pipeline that supplied her material.

She dressed meticulously in a black wool skirt and rose heather sweater, with high black boots and a print challis shawl. When she went downstairs, Neil and Connor were sitting in the living room with Adrienne and Matthew, and Connor held baby Hailey.

"Kate, we've been doing some follow-up on the Burton family, and it looks like you were right. Jim Burton is still in town, or at least, he's not far away."

"Thanks for telling me. I guess you don't want him to know that you know, huh?"

"That's right. I can't say much, but I didn't want you to think I don't value what you gave us yesterday. We've been looking into it, and I believe he's been in touch with his family. But that's just between us."

"Okay."

Neil had stood and was waiting for her. As they put on their coats, Kate resolved not to ask him any questions about the case that afternoon. She didn't have to work again until Monday, and if the case split wide open this weekend and they caught Jim Burton, she would let someone else write it. But somehow she didn't think things were moving too fast. Neil was taking her to visit Oma as scheduled, and Connor was relaxing at home in jeans and a T-shirt. If he thought he would be rushing out on business, he wouldn't be so laid-back.

On their drive to the Pines, she held the small container of cookies she had brought as a gift for the older woman. Neil asked her about her father's farm in Skowhegan, and she got him to tell her a little more about his family.

"Will you pray for them, Kate? My folks seem to think they're all right spiritually, because they're nice people. But they don't understand that's not enough. They need Jesus."

She felt tears rush into her eyes. "I will. From what you've told me, you've tried hard to get that across."

"Maybe too hard. The last time I said something to my sister Anneke, she told me she doesn't want me to talk about it around her anymore, so I don't very much."

"I'll ask God to bring the right opportunity," Kate said. "Maybe He'll bring someone else along to share the gospel with them. Sometimes families don't want to hear it from their own."

Neil reached over and squeezed her hand. "Thanks. I can't quit trying. So, did you get the rest of your boxes moved this morning?"

"No. I called, and Madyson wasn't home. I left a message, but she only called me back an hour ago, and there wasn't time. I'll have to get them Monday before work, I guess." Kate shook her head. "She made it sound like it was urgent, and now I can't connect with her."

When they reached the retirement home, Oma Alexander was waiting for them in the large lounge. Neil took Kate's hand and led her forward.

"*Dag,* Oma." He bent down to kiss the old woman's cheek. "I'd like you to meet Kate Richards."

"Sit, sit." Oma's plump pink cheeks jiggled as she patted the seat beside her on the sofa. Her white hair was arranged in a braid, pulled to the back of her head. "I have heard about you."

"You have?" Kate looked up at Neil, but he just grinned and sat down in an armchair nearby.

"Oh, *ja,* my grandson is close with his personal life, but he tells me things now and then."

Kate smiled and held out the small, decorative box. "I brought you something."

Oma took the box and lifted the cover. "Ah, Cornelius must have told you I have a sweet tooth. *Dank je.*"

"I'll carry it down to your room for you after we talk, Oma," Neil said.

Kate settled back against the firm cushions. "How long have you lived in Maine, Mrs. Alexander?"

Neil's grandmother waved her hand and crinkled up her face. "Call me Oma."

"All right. Thank you…Oma."

"I have been here a long time. Too long."

"Oh? Do you miss the Netherlands?"

"*Ja,* I don't like all this snow and ice. We had snow in Holland, but not like this. But it will pass."

A woman pushed a tea cart into the room, and Neil said, "Oma, would you like some tea?"

"*Dank je,*" said Oma with a nod.

"Kate?"

"Yes, please."

"He's a good boy," his grandmother whispered when he'd turned his back. "He is very serious about his work and his religion."

"Yes, he's dedicated to both," Kate agreed.

"My daughter-in-law, Hendrika, she thinks he is *niet gezellig.*"

Kate frowned.

Oma chuckled and patted her hand. "He doesn't do what his family would like, you know. He missed her big dinner Christmas Day, for one. And he wouldn't stay late to play cards that night." She shook her head, smiling. "The holidays are very important to the Dutch, you know. But perhaps he knows what is really important, *nee?*"

Kate smiled. "I think you may be right. Oma, would you mind if I asked you some questions about Holland and wrote down your answers? I'd like to write a story about you and how you came to live here."

"Cornelius told me you are a writer for the biggest paper in all of Maine."

"Yes, that's true."

"But you don't want to put me in the paper."

"Why not?" Kate asked.

"You think people want to read about an old woman?"

"Yes, I do. I know you have some wonderful memories of Holland. Neil told me how you used to skate to school, and how your father owned a dairy near an old castle."

"Oh, *ja,* that was a long time ago." Neil handed Oma her teacup, and she settled back in her seat. "If you really want to hear…"

"I most certainly do." Already Kate could envision her feature story with a picture of the darling old woman in the Sunday leisure section. Chatting with Oma was almost enough to distract her from thinking about the murders and the fugitive the police were hunting.

That evening, she sat in the truck and closed her eyes as Neil drove her home. The day had been perfect. Well, from two o'clock on. Tea with Oma. Perusing her photos of the Netherlands. Dinner with Neil, followed by the magnificent show at the Civic Center. This day went beyond her most lavish imaginings. She felt Neil's hand on hers and looked over at him.

"Not sleeping, are you?" he asked softly.

"No, just…fixing the memories." She wrapped her fingers in his and felt the delicious warmth of his hand.

"The horses were great, weren't they?"

She smiled. "I wasn't thinking about the horses."

When they arrived at the Larson home, he hopped out, and she made herself sit and pull her gloves on while he walked around the truck and opened the door for her.

"Thanks."

They walked up to the breezeway together. A cold wind cut across the neighborhood, whistling down the street. Kate shivered.

"Come in for a minute?"

Neil shrugged. "Looks like they've buttoned down for the night."

Kate tried the doorknob, but the door was locked. She pulled her key ring out and unlocked the door.

"Good night," Neil said. Their eyes met, and he slowly leaned down and gently grazed her lips with his.

She smiled and put her gloved hand up to his cheek. "Thank you, for everything, Neil. Good night." With a little wave, Kate slipped through the front door and closed it softly behind her.

On Monday morning, Kate left the house early, determined to retrieve her boxes from the old apartment across town before going to the office. The idyllic weekend, which had included church and Sunday dinner with Adrienne's family and Neil, had almost lulled her into thinking she could happily live a quiet life.

But today she was back in high gear, ready to ferret out another front-page story. Something big was out there waiting for her to discover it; she could feel it.

She headed her car into the West End of town, toward the apartment. Madyson came to the door yawning, wearing only her nightshirt.

"I'm sorry," Kate said. "I'm on my way to work. I'll just get my stuff and get out of your hair."

She quickly loaded her three cartons of books and tapes and headed back toward Congress Street. As she passed a pancake house, her eye was drawn to a tall young man getting out of a vehicle. She started to brake, but restrained the impulse and

glided past. When she was sure she was out of sight, she pulled
into a parking lot and turned around. She went back to the restaurant and drove in. The car was still there, and she glimpsed
a familiar figure in the driver's seat. Her pulse quickened, and
she nosed into a parking spot and lunged for her cell phone.

"Neil! I just saw Stephen Burton go into a pancake restaurant, and his father is sitting outside in a car." She leaned forward
as she gave him her location, trying to see through the windows
of the vehicles between her car and Burton's.

"Kate, get out of there," Neil said. "Stephen will recognize
you if he sees you."

"He went in alone. Do you think he's meeting someone?"

"He's probably getting breakfast for his father. Jim Burton
can't show his face in public. His picture's been all over the
media, as you well know. Can you be seen from the entrance?
How about through the windows?"

"Uh...probably." She swallowed hard. "I can duck if he
comes out."

"Look, I've got Connor and Tony. We're on our way. Just
drive on out, and keep driving. Go to work, and I'll call you
later."

"But I won't—"

"No, Kate! Listen to me. You mean too much to me. If something happens to you because of your stubbornness, I don't know
what I'd do. Plus, you might blow our best chance of nabbing
Burton. Now get moving before Stephen comes out and spots you."

He hung up, and she stared at her phone. "I can't believe he
hung up on me. Of course, he did admit that he cares."

Movement caught her eye then, and she glanced toward the
restaurant. Her heart did a handspring. Stephen Burton was
coming out the door, and she was certain he looked her way. He
kept walking toward his father's car, balancing a paper bag and
a tray containing two covered cups.

She sat still, afraid to move a muscle. When he was out of
her vision between the cars, she exhaled. He must not have seen

her, or at least he hadn't recognized her. Now what? She couldn't drive out or he might notice her. Had he seen her car the day she'd interviewed him? Impossible to be sure. She decided to sit tight until they drove out. If they left before the police arrived, she could watch and see which way they went.

Pulling out her notebook, she jotted the name of the restaurant and its location. She tried again to see the other car, but an SUV between them was higher and blocked her view. Stretching, she lifted her head and sat tall. She could see just a bit of the dark green car's roofline. They must be sitting in the car, eating their food. It struck her that if she could take a picture of the car on her cell phone, it might help the police.

No, that would be stupid. Neil would never speak to her again, for sure.

Even as she rejected the thought, her hand closed on the door handle. The latch unhooked, but before she could open the door, more people came out of the restaurant. She froze and looked away, but suddenly she realized the people were headed for the SUV next to her car. After they got in and pulled away, she took a quick look to her right. With only one car left between them, she had a clear view of the green car. She could see Stephen sitting in the front passenger seat, sipping his drink and looking forward, toward the restaurant. The driver's seat was empty.

Kate felt suddenly cold inside. Where was Jim Burton? A sudden instinct told her to close and lock her door. She started to swing it open so she could slam it, but something held it back. She looked up to see Jim Burton—or rather, Joseph Parlin—as he restrained her door, holding it open six inches. He was wearing the toupee and the brown contact lenses. The thought skimmed through her mind as she lowered her gaze and focused on the muzzle of the small handgun he was pointing straight at her.

"Miss Richards, I'm a big fan. I've been following your articles for a couple of weeks now. Won't you join my son and me for coffee?"

FIFTEEN

"We'll owe Kate big-time if we can get Burton this morning," Connor said as they sped down Congress Street in Neil's pickup. "Roberta Palmer's finally got the picture that she and Jim Burton are not going to retire together."

"Is the district attorney going to cut her a deal?" Neil asked, keeping an eye on Tony's Mustang in his rearview mirror.

"Sounds like it. When I told her we managed to keep Burton from getting the building fund money he had transferred and spelled out her options for her, she told me how they planned this thing."

"Even the murders?" Neil asked.

"Yeah. She wanted to make sure we knew she didn't pull the trigger. She heard Ted telling Edna something was wrong, and that he thought Mr. Burton was a bad apple."

"Just a vague suspicion?"

"No, apparently Ted had heard Burton say something incriminating. Roberta wasn't exactly sure how much he knew, but she insists he knew about their plans. He looked daggers at her all morning, and she eavesdropped on him and Edna while they were bathing the puppies. She heard Ted say the Society had better not trust Burton, and that he thought he had his eye on the building fund. That was on Christmas Eve. Roberta went straight to Jim. They tried to come up with some way to stop the two from telling anyone else. Jim wasn't sure what they could do, but he improvised a way to get their house keys. Roberta told them that the parking lot was going to be plowed, and she'd move their cars for them. They both handed over their key rings. She went and moved their cars to the other side of the lot, and Jim went out and took the keys from her. She avoided Edna and Ted for an hour or so, and Jim brought the keys back. Then she went in all apologetic and returned them. Made an excuse, like she'd had to run to the bank or something."

"That's why the houses were locked when the bodies were discovered," Neil said. "He made copies of their house keys."

"Yes. He didn't really need to go to all that trouble. Both volunteers would probably have let him in anyway, but he wanted to get inside without alerting their families, I guess."

"Except Ted Hepburn lived alone."

"Right. Just him and the four cats. Roberta insists she didn't know Burton was going to kill Ted and Edna, didn't even think he planned to do it. Just a spur-of-the-moment thing, she said."

"Oh, I've heard that one before," Neil said. " 'Please, Mr. Detective, I didn't mean to do it. I just took my gun along to scare him with it.' Give me a break."

"Yeah, well, it might work for one murder, but not two," said Connor. "And you don't have your victim's house keys copied if you only intend to scare him a little. Roberta said he told her afterward that he couldn't think of any other solution. Roberta said she was appalled."

"Naturally." Neil shook his head. "So appalled she ran right to the police and told them her boyfriend, with whom she was planning to steal upward of a million dollars, had just killed two people."

"That's my take, too," said Connor. "At least she's ready to testify against him now."

"What if he says she did it?" Neil asked. He'd seen a murder case like that, where two people blamed each other, and they both walked.

"I think we've got him," Connor said. "Stephen saw him cleaning the gun, and he got Roberta to mail him the cash. He personally emptied the building fund accounts. We've got enough to keep him in jail a long, long time."

"Well, I hope we can make the murder charges stick." Neil drove in the front entrance of the pancake house's parking lot as Tony gunned his Mustang in the side entrance.

"Green car," Neil said to Connor. "Where is it?"

Connor scanned the lot, gritting his teeth. "Not here. We've lost them."

On the other side of the lot, Tony eased along the row of cars.

"Stop!" Connor clawed at his seat belt.

"What?"

"That's Kate's car." He jerked his chin toward a red compact sedan.

Neil looked. A wave of sickness tossed his stomach. Connor threw off the belt and yanked his door open. Neil slammed the gearshift into Park and jumped out. Connor was already opening the driver's door of Kate's car.

Tony pulled up and lowered his window. "I thought you said it was a green car."

"That's Kate's car," Neil told him. "She didn't leave when I told her to. Check in the restaurant and see if she's inside."

Tony bounded from his seat, leaving his treasured Mustang idling in the traffic lane of the parking lot.

Connor straightened and shut the car door. "The passenger door is locked, but this one wasn't."

"She got out on her own." Neil managed a half smile. "Hey, she's probably close by."

Connor shook his head. "This was on the floor near the gas pedal."

He held up Kate's phone.

Kate huddled against the door in the backseat of Jim Burton's car, as far away from him as she could get. Burton sat beside her, pointing the gun at her midsection while his son drove.

"Too bad you had to be so nosy," Burton said. "When Stephen

told me you were watching us, I couldn't just drive off and leave you there. You would go to the police. I can't have that happen until we tie up a few loose ends."

"Until you get your money, you mean? I know they blocked your foreign bank account, Mr. Burton. There's no way you'll get that building fund money. Ever."

He scowled. "Stephen told me you were asking him all kinds of questions about me Friday. He thought he didn't spill anything important, but I guess he was wrong. Have you been following him, or did he tell you where I was?"

"Neither."

"Right."

"It's true. I took a different route to work this morning, and I just happened to be driving past the pancake house when Stephen got out of your car."

"As if I'd believe that."

Kate clamped her lips together and looked out the window. Stephen turned onto Forest Avenue, and she wondered where they were going. Not Jim and Claire Burton's home.

A few minutes later, Stephen parked on a side street.

"We'll wait here," Burton said, still holding the gun on Kate.

"You know they won't give it to me," Stephen said. "They wouldn't give it to Sean."

"That was Saturday. There'll be a different clerk on today. Wait until there are several people in line. When it's busy. You just never know."

Stephen got out of the car. Kate watched him cross the street. They waited nearly ten minutes in silence. She wondered if Burton would shoot if she opened the door and ran. *Lord, give me wisdom.* Her heart sank as she saw Stephen walking down the sidewalk empty-handed.

He opened the car door and slid into the driver's seat. "They won't give it to me. They asked for ID."

"Did you show them any?"

"No. I said my father would come and get the package."

Burton swore. "Did you see any cops?"

"No. But there are a lot of cars in the front parking lot."

"I guess it's the only way." Burton raised the gun a couple of inches, drawing Kate's attention to it. "Miss Richards, I'll have this in my pocket, pointed at you every second. Walk slightly ahead of me and go in the side entrance of the post office. Get in the shortest line. And don't even think about yelling or trying to run. I won't hesitate to shoot."

Kate began to tremble. "Can't I stay here with Stephen?"

"No. I need a guarantee that I'll leave the post office alive. You are my insurance. Now get out on the sidewalk, and remember—I'm right behind you."

Tony ran out of the restaurant. "She's not in there."

"You sure?" Neil called.

"Positive. Ask the ladies in the restroom how I know."

Connor was already on his radio with the dispatcher. "Send four units to Jim and Claire Burton's house." He gave the address. "And we've got to watch the interstate south."

"You think he's back with the wife?" Tony asked.

Neil shrugged. "He's got both his boys running errands for him. And Mrs. B was in deep denial about the murders last week. Maybe he's convinced her Roberta did it and set him up."

Connor yelled, "Come on, let's move."

Tony opened the door of his Mustang. "Burton's house?"

"I don't know where else to look," Connor said. "You think we should send a unit to the animal shelter?"

"The post office," Neil said. "They were getting breakfast while they waited for the window to open at the post office."

Connor met his gaze and slowly nodded. "Right. Emily is back on duty this morning. Let's go."

Neil jumped into his truck. Tony slapped a blue light on the top of his Mustang and roared out of the parking lot.

They were halfway to the post office when the dispatcher called Connor. His features tightened as he took the call.

"All right, send as many uniforms as you can. Now." He turned to Neil. "Emily just notified dispatch. Jim Burton is at the post office wearing the Parlin disguise, and there's a woman with him. He handed in the card for the package, and Emily's stalling him."

Neil flipped on his flashing blue light and siren. Connor grimaced and clapped his hands over his ears, but didn't complain.

Kate stood beside Burton before the post office counter, trying to keep her face impassive. Burton's occasional nudge in her side and his stony expression kept her pulse thundering.

"Here you go, Mr. Parlin," said the clerk, setting a white box on the counter. "Sorry about the delay. Just sign right here, please."

"What for?"

"This package was insured."

Burton hesitated. That must not have been in the plan, Kate thought. He scrawled something on the form the clerk handed him and tossed down the pen.

"Thanks." He tucked the package under his arm and nodded to Kate. She turned toward the door, her mind racing. Now, if ever, was the time to act, while he was distracted and had the package to deal with. He'd gone to a lot of trouble to get it, and she was pretty sure he wouldn't want to let go of that, no matter what.

When she opened the post office door, she heard sirens in the distance and hesitated. Burton swore. He stepped close to her and put his arm around her.

"My gun is right under your rib, darling. Don't try anything. Just walk quickly with me to the car." As they reached the curb, there was a slight break in traffic. "Go now."

Kate's breath came in shallow gasps as she hastened across the street. A few more steps, and she could see the green car, parked around the corner. The volume of the sirens surged, and a dark car pulled in next to the sidewalk, a few feet ahead of

them. Burton stopped, and Kate darted another glance toward
the car they had arrived in. Stephen started the green car moving,
just as a red Mustang turned the corner and swung in front of it.
She winced as metal crunched metal.

Burton's arm clamped her hard against his side, and he swung
her around. The siren volume was painful now. A black pickup
drove toward them with a blue strobe flashing on the dashboard.
She recognized Neil and Connor as the truck jumped the curb
and hit the sidewalk. She opened her mouth to scream. He would
never stop in time on the snowy sidewalk.

Burton jumped back, pulling her with him, and Kate shoved
him hard. They both went down into the snowbank that edged the
sidewalk. She thrust herself away from him and struggled to
stand.

Strong hands seized her from behind and lifted her.

"Put you hands up, Burton."

She saw Connor reach down and retrieve Burton's handgun
from the snow.

"Kate, are you all right?"

She whirled around and realized Neil was the one who had
pulled her away from Jim Burton. She stared into his face for a
moment, unable to form words. He hauled her in against the
front of his jacket and wrapped his arms around her.

"It's okay. You're okay."

She closed her eyes and leaned against him, shaking.

"Come sit in the truck," Neil said.

Her knees quivered uncontrollably as they went the few steps,
and he opened the door for her.

"In you go." He dashed to the driver's side, got in, killed the
siren and turned the heater up as high as it would go.

Kate drew in a deep breath and tried to stop her lips from
trembling. "I'm surprised you're still speaking to me."

His eyebrows shot up. "Kate, how can you—"

"You said I was stubborn, and you were right."

Comprehension dawned in his eyes. "Did I say stubborn?"

I meant tenacious." He reached for her and pulled her against his shoulder.

She closed her eyes and squeezed him. "Do you need to be out there?"

"We've got at least twenty cops on it. I think Connor would want me to keep an eye on you."

She opened her eyes and sat up, squinting out at the sun-on-snow glare. Burton was handcuffed, and two uniformed officers held him while Connor read him his rights. Tony Carlisle was frisking Stephen, who stood with his hands on top of his father's car. The Mustang's front left fender was melded to that of the green sedan.

"Poor Tony."

"Yeah," Neil murmured, kissing her hair. "He really shouldn't drive that Mustang to work."

Kate turned toward him, and he kissed her gently but with an underlying hint of passion she knew she no longer wanted to live without.

SIXTEEN

On Tuesday, Neil took Kate home after an evening with his parents. This time the lights were still blazing, and he went in with her.

"Connor and Adri are still up, I guess," he said.

"Probably Hailey's keeping them awake."

They went into the living room and found their hosts sitting together on the couch, watching a movie.

"Well, hi! Did you have a good time?" Adrienne asked as Connor paused the video.

Neil kept quiet and watched Kate. He was sort of wondering the same thing. He'd already apologized in the truck for his brother-in-law Dennis's unrestrained drinking.

Kate's mile-wide smile had to be genuine. "It was great. I love Neil's parents. We played games and ate a ton of snacks. I think we're *gezellig* now."

Neil laughed. "Not quite. We left too early for that. To be really in with a Dutch family, you have to be the last one to leave the game table." He looked at Connor. "So, any new developments?"

"Nope. I'm off-duty, and I unplugged the phone."

"Do you want some coffee?" Adrienne asked.

"No, thanks. I'd better get going," Neil said.

"Right. You need to be at the courthouse early in the morning for Jim Burton's arraignment," Connor reminded him.

Neil nodded. "Will do."

"I don't understand his wife," Kate said. "Her husband left

her for another woman, robbed his employer and killed two people. But she still agreed to help him skip town and set up a new life somewhere else with their two sons."

"I don't get it, either," said Connor.

"It's very simple," said Adrienne.

"It is?" He stared at her.

"She's taken him back. Probably made him grovel first."

"But the thefts, and the murders," Neil said.

"You guys said she won't admit he did the murders," Adrienne pointed out.

"No, but she knows they were committed with his gun," said Connor.

"She told me someone else must have used his gun, that Jim wasn't capable of doing it," Neil said. "She claimed he was being set up."

Adrienne nodded. "Some women will forgive a lot for security."

"You wouldn't," said Connor.

"Maybe not something like that," she agreed. "But if he spun a good enough story, seemed truly penitent and promised her a good life together…"

"Maybe he's sworn off other women and told her he'll take her and the boys someplace where they can live happily ever after," Kate speculated.

"Maybe he really thought he could," Neil said. "Get the money and get his family back, too."

Kate walked him back to the entry. "Thanks so much, Neil. I hope your family wasn't too disappointed in me."

"No way. I think Mama was favorably impressed, and Papa obviously adores you."

"Well, I like them. But you've got to give me some pointers on bluffing."

"You did all right at games. I just wondered about the rest of it. I know you're used to a Christian family."

Her smile softened. "Who says they won't join us one day?"

He folded her in against his chest. "Thank you. Tonight was…"

"What?"

"I want to say perfect, but it wasn't. I mean, if there hadn't been any beer, and my papa wouldn't swear so much…but…Kate, being with you makes me feel like everything's right in spite of the things that aren't. You know what I mean?"

"Yeah, I think I do." She reached up to his collar and adjusted it. Neil looked deep into her eyes and leaned down to kiss her. She emerged from his embrace with a glowing smile. He'd never looked into a woman's eyes before and seen such trust and longing and joy.

"I'll call you tomorrow." He squeezed her briefly and went out.

The next day Neil left the courthouse shortly before noon. He dropped Tony off at the body shop to pick up his gently restored Mustang, grabbed a burger and drove back to the police station.

"So, was Claire Burton in on it?" Connor asked him after he'd reported on the arraignment.

"I don't know. The D.A. is trying to work that one out. Jim Burton's stacked up enough charges to keep him in prison for life. Stephen has been charged as an accessory to kidnapping Kate and various other counts. Sean, I'm afraid, will have it hard."

"He's not being charged?" Connor asked.

"No, but it's possible his mother may be. I'm hoping Sean can go to his grandparents in New Jersey. Otherwise, it's foster care."

"Tough on a kid that age," Connor said.

"Yes, I feel bad for him. He's not a hard kid, really."

"He will be after this."

Neil's cell phone rang. He pulled it from his pocket. "Marianne." He put the phone to his ear. "Hey, sis, what's up?"

"It's Oma. The Pines just called Mama. They think she had a stroke or something. They're taking her to Maine Medical."

"I'll be right there."

"Okay. I'm here with Mama, but I think she and Papa will go over as soon as he gets here from work. And I called Anneke. She may get there before we do."

"What is it?" asked Connor as Neil closed his phone.

"My Oma. They just took her to the hospital."

"Go on," Connor said. "Don't even think about coming back to work today."

At the hospital, Neil found his sister Anneke weeping in the emergency room's waiting area.

"They said I can go in soon," she told him, dabbing at her eyes with a tissue.

Neil put his arms around her. "Is Dennis coming?"

"I tried to call him, but he's out on the truck," she said. Dennis worked for a cable company and spent a lot of time out on the road. "He'll be off in a couple of hours, so I decided to just wait. We'll know how she is by then."

A uniformed woman came in from the examining area and asked for Mrs. Alexander's family. Anneke and Neil followed her through a double door, around a triage desk, to an exam room.

Oma looked very small, lying on the stretcher with a white sheet covering her up to her chest. She had on a paisley blouse she wore a lot, and her white hair was braided as usual, but her face was pale. Her eyes were closed, and her mouth was a little slack, drooping on the right side. Her hands lay limply on top of the sheet.

"I'm Dr. Pelkey," said a woman standing near the bed. She was fifty or so, with short brown hair and glasses. She wore a long white jacket over a peach dress, and a stethoscope hung around her neck.

"We're her grandchildren. I'm Neil Alexander, and this is my sister, Anneke West."

"You grandmother has had a stroke," the doctor said. "We're not sure yet to what extent it has affected her. There seem to be some speech and motor problems. We've done a couple of initial tests, but we'll need to do more. Who would be able to give permission for that?"

"My father, I guess," Neil said. "He'll be here soon."

"All right, I think we'll proceed," Dr. Pelkey said. "Time is important in a case like this."

Anneke reached to hold Oma's hand. Oma's eyes flickered.

"Can she hear me?" Anneke asked the doctor.

"She might be able to. It certainly wouldn't hurt if you would speak to her. I'm going to set up the next tests, and I'll be back in just a few minutes."

She left the room, and Neil went around to the other side of the stretcher and patted Oma's hair.

"Oma," said Anneke, "can you hear me?"

She spoke in Dutch, which Anneke seldom did anymore, and it touched Neil that she did now, bringing it home to him how serious this was. He prayed silently.

His parents and Marianne arrived a few minutes later, and he and Anneke went out into the waiting area to give them space in the small exam room.

"You should call Kate," Anneke said.

Neil hesitated. "Do you think so? You wouldn't mind?"

"Of course not. You care about her a lot. That was obvious last night."

Kate answered on the first ring, and her warm voice steadied him.

"Are you all right?" she asked. "Connor called me about Oma. How is she?"

"I'm fine, but Oma… They don't think she'll make it."

"I'm so sorry."

Neil sniffed and looked around the waiting room for a box of tissues. "It's hard, Kate."

"I know. Do you want me to come down there?" she asked.

"I…don't want to ask you to do that. Just pray for her, and for me."

"I can come. I'd like to, if you want me to."

It was what he'd hoped to hear, and he exhaled in relief. "Thank you. I'd really like that." He gave her directions and went back to sit with Anneke.

After about twenty minutes, Marianne came out and told them the nurses were taking Oma upstairs to a hospital room on the medical-surgical floor. Neil waited downstairs for Kate, and the rest of the family went up to another waiting room.

Kate entered through the door Neil had directed her to. He pulled her into his arms in the hallway and held her close. "Thank you."

"It's going to be okay." She stroked his hair. "How are you holding up?"

"Better now."

They went up the elevator and found his sisters.

"Hello, Kate." Anneke kissed her on the cheek. "Mama and Papa are in Oma's room now."

They sat down together and talked quietly about Oma. Neil held Kate's hand. Every time he got that scary, tight feeling in his chest, he looked at her, and her empathetic blue eyes centered him.

About three o'clock, Marianne's husband, Marc, arrived, then Dennis. The nurse came out and said they could go into Oma's room, two at a time. Neil told the girls to go first, and waited with Kate, Marc and Dennis.

Fifteen minutes later, Mama came to the waiting area and told Neil to come. "Oh, hello, Kate."

Kate stood. "Hello, Mrs. Alexander. I'm so sorry."

"Thank you." Mama turned her attention back to Neil. "She's tried to speak."

"What did she say?" he asked.

"Mostly, nothing we can understand. But she said your father's name, and I thought she said 'Cornelius,' so I came to get you."

Kate squeezed his hand. "I'll wait here."

He nodded and followed his mother down the hall. An IV line ran into Oma's left hand, and she lay pale and vulnerable in the bed. She was wearing a hospital johnny. Her eyes were open, and her breathing seemed labored.

"She wants you," Marianne said between sobs. She hugged Neil and went out into the hall. Papa sat gravely beside the bed, holding his mother's hand. Neil went to the other side, and Anneke moved aside for him.

"Cornelius."

"I'm here, Oma." He touched her hand. Her mouth twitched, and they sat for a long time.

Three different doctors came in and looked at her, checked her reflexes and tried to get her to respond to them verbally. By five o'clock, they had decided to leave her alone until early morning.

Dr. Pelkey said, "She may not make it through tonight. If she's strong enough in the morning, we'll do more tests, but there's really not much we can do right now. Sometimes they rally, but this seems pretty massive, and she hasn't responded to the drug therapy we gave her when she came in."

Neil went out to the waiting room. "I think I should stay here tonight with Mama and Papa," he told Kate.

"Do you mind if I wait out here?"

"You don't have to."

"I want to. I called Adri and Connor to let them knew."

Marc and Dennis took his sisters to collect their children from the friends who were watching them. Kate rounded up a stack of magazines and settled down in the otherwise deserted waiting room.

"Are you sure?" Neil said.

"Positive. I'll be right here any time you want to talk."

He kissed her and went back to Oma's room.

Mama and Papa stayed. The hospital settled into nighttime routine. Oma lay unmoving, her eyes closed, the only sounds coming from the monitors and Oma's shallow breaths.

Finally, Neil's mother said to her husband, "You'd better eat something, Paul."

"No, no."

"Yes, you should. You haven't eaten since noon."

"All right," he said after a moment. "We'll go downstairs and see what we can get to eat."

"The coffee shop might still be open," Mama said. "How about you, Neil? Are you hungry?"

"Bring me a sandwich and some coffee." He took out his wallet. "Do you mind getting Kate something, too? Black coffee."

"Put your money away," said his father, and they went out.

Neil took the little Bible Connor and Adrienne had given him from his jacket pocket and opened to the Psalms. He read through Psalm 37, and it was a comfort to him, but it made him fear for Oma's soul. He turned to Romans.

"Cornelius." Oma's voice sounded faint.

He leaned toward her quickly. "*Ja,* Oma?"

Her eyes were open, and they found his face, but her head hadn't moved.

"Oma, do you want to say something to me?" He grasped her hand.

"I'm afraid."

Tears started in Neil's eyes. "You don't have to be afraid. Just trust Jesus to save you. Jesus is the one who died for our sins."

She looked up at him blankly.

"Just trust Jesus," Neil said. "You don't have to do anything else. He did everything, Oma." He struggled mentally with his rusty Dutch and decided he didn't have the words to say what he wanted to tell her. He turned in his Bible to John 1 and looked at verse 12. "If you receive Jesus Christ and believe in His name, He will save you."

Her eyes flickered.

"We can't do anything to deserve eternal life," Neil said. "All we can do is believe in Jesus."

"Jesus," she whispered hoarsely.

"*Ja,* Oma. He did everything on the cross. Just trust Him."

She closed her eyes. Neil grabbed a tissue from the box on

the nightstand and wiped his eyes. He sat and prayed, wondering if he'd said it right and if she'd understood.

His folks came back a little while later, and brought him a hamburger meal. He set it on the nightstand, but his mother said, "Eat, eat," so he took the sandwich out and unwrapped it.

"How is she?" Papa asked, sitting down heavily in his chair on the other side of the bed.

"She spoke to me."

"What did she say?" Mama asked.

Neil hesitated. "She said my name first, and then she said she was afraid."

Tears spilled from his father's eyes and dropped down onto the front of his shirt.

"I told her to trust Jesus," Neil said. "The last thing she said was…'Jesus.'"

His father closed his eyes. Neil prayed again in silence, holding Oma's hand, and his mother sat silent, too.

His grandmother's breath came slower, and each one seemed a gasp. Neil wished he could call his pastor, but he thought his parents would be offended.

"Kate is still waiting," his mother said. "She's a nice girl, Neil."

"Thanks. I know."

"She's good for you," Papa said.

Neil smiled and wiped at the tears.

The nurse came in and checked the readings on Oma's monitor. She walked over to Papa and laid a hand on his sleeve. "I don't think it will be long, Mr. Alexander."

Mama stood. "I'll go and call the girls." She and the nurse left the room.

Neil rounded the bed and sat down beside Papa. After a moment, Papa turned and opened his arms. Neil hugged him. They cried together for a minute. When Papa pulled away, Neil sat back and watched Oma.

Every time she pulled in a breath, he thought it was the last.

She hung on until Marc brought Marianne and Anneke in. Marianne was crying uncontrollably, and Marc kept his arm around her. Anneke said they'd left all the children with Dennis. She sat, white-faced, her eyes not leaving Oma's face.

Oma gasped one more spasmodic breath. Neil waited for the next one, but it didn't come.

Kate's eyelids drooped, and she set the magazine aside. It was after midnight. Maybe she should go home. She sent up another prayer for Oma and all of Neil's family. *Lord, is it really best for me to be here? I can't do anything for them.*

Quiet footsteps approached, and she looked up to see Neil in the doorway, his face bathed in tears. She sprang up and pulled him into the room and put her arms around him.

"Neil, I'm so sorry."

"I talked to her when Mama and Papa were gone. I told her to trust Jesus. She said His name. Kate, I think she believed."

"I hope you're right." She stroked his shoulders. "We'll know when we get to heaven."

His arms tightened around her. He clung to her for a long minute with his forehead against her temple, breathing raggedly and caressing her hair.

"Thank you." He eased gently away. "Come sit down a minute. Papa's talking to the nurse about arrangements." They settled in on the vinyl-covered sofa. "My folks will go to the funeral home tomorrow, but I expect the service will be Friday."

"I'll be there," Kate said. "And Adri and I will bring dinner for your family tomorrow. I already talked to her, and we want to do that so your mother doesn't have to cook."

Neil smiled gently. "Thank you. You'll be *gezellig* for sure, after this."

"And Connor says he doesn't expect you to work the rest of the week."

Neil wrapped his arms around her and pulled her against his shoulder. "Kate, I don't want to wait anymore to say this. I love you. I've never felt this way about anyone before. Like I want to be with you always. For the rest of my life."

Kate's pulse raced, but her rational mind whispered, "Caution." She leaned back and eyed him carefully. "Neil, you're not proposing, are you? Because it's way too soon, you know."

"No," he said. "I just want you to know that I love you, and you're the woman I want to grow old with."

Kate gulped and brushed back the hair that shadowed his eyes. "I love you, too, Neil."

Neil lowered his head and gave her a lingering kiss.

After a long moment, he lifted his head and stared deeply into Kate's eyes.

"You're right, you know." He leaned back against the sofa. "This can't be a proposal, because when I propose it will be much better than this. Moonlight and roses and music, you know, the whole shebang. Fireworks, even."

She smiled. "Fireworks?"

"Oh, yeah. Which are hard to arrange in Maine without getting arrested. But for now—well, I love you, Kate. And…and you said you love me."

"I do."

"That's enough for now, I guess."

She eased back into his embrace. "Yes, it's plenty for now. I'll look forward to the rest."

She felt a sudden longing for the Fourth of July.

* * * * *

Dear Reader,

This story is different from those I usually tell. Kate, the heroine, is young and idealistic. Like many of us, when she met a handsome, charming man, she assumed everything else about him was good, too. By the time she faced the fact that Neil didn't respect her faith or her convictions, her heart was already entangled. Though she managed to turn back to God and break the relationship, she left Neil confused and both of them hurt. By God's grace, Neil found Christ, and the Lord opened a new door for them. Understandably, both were hesitant to enter that doorway.

Kate's other main conflict—her ambition—is one we all face. The exhilaration of success led her to push people for favors when she shouldn't have. Learning to leave selfishness behind and balance her work and her relationships is difficult, but Kate was well on the way by the end of this story.

Neil's relationship with his family was strained because he accepted a faith they didn't understand. His parents were disappointed because he didn't meet their expectations. Even for a grown man, that's hard to take. Resolution for Neil came at his grandmother's hospital bedside, with hope that his family will now be more open to hearing his witness.

The difficulties these two face—pride, ambition, attraction to the wrong person and family conflicts, are ones many Christians face. I hope that traveling this journey with Kate and Neil will lift you up as you face variations of these problems in your own life. May God bless you as you seek to draw closer to Him.

I love hearing from my readers. Come visit me on my Web site at www.susanpagedavis.com.

Susan Page Davis

QUESTIONS FOR DISCUSSION

1. Kate leaves her parents' home when making the jump from a small-town weekly newspaper to a city daily paper. How does her determination to succeed in her new job affect her relationship with others?

2. Why does Neil's family feel so uneasy with his choice to believe in Christ? Have you ever found it difficult to share your faith with a family member? How did you handle it?

3. Adrienne and Connor introduced Neil and Kate, but regretted it after the two wound up hurting each other. When Kate returns to Portland, they don't tell Neil she's back—at Kate's request. Have you put off facing someone or some issue that has caused you grief in the past? How do you feel about the way Kate handled reconnecting with Neil?

4. When Connor takes vacation to be with Adrienne and the baby, Neil is overwhelmed by the prospect of being "in charge" at the office. What steps does he take to help him fulfill his responsibilities? Does being a leader or a manager scare you? How do you deal with it?

5. In addition to gathering information for her articles, Kate has to learn to guard what she tells others. Is keeping a confidence difficult for you? What guidelines do you use to know when it's okay to pass on information?

6. Oma is perhaps the first person who listens to Neil's witness without shutting the conversation down. Yet Neil can't know for sure that she understood and received Christ. What would you tell Neil after this experience?

7. What devices does Roberta Palmer use to cover her role in the embezzlement? Have you ever been shocked to learn someone you considered a nice person is not so nice? How did you deal with it in your own heart?

8. How has Connor helped Neil and Kate grow in their spiritual and social lives?

9. During the ice storm and after Oma's stroke, Adrienne jumps into action to help others. What have you done to help friends or strangers during a crisis? Where would you draw the line on helping others, or is there a line at all?

10. Kate could have driven away from the restaurant after she alerted Neil about Jim Burton's presence. What stopped her? How did her impulsiveness and ambition lead her into trouble? What verse or biblical principle could you use as guidance in a dangerous situation?

11. Neil has a checkered past in his social life. Should Kate have waited longer to accept the "new Neil"? Would you immediately accept a new Christian who left a life of sin, or would you sit back and wait to watch his progress? How would you encourage the new believer as he struggled to leave his old life behind?

12. Connor sets boundaries for his men and for Kate. Neil is his subordinate but also accepts his limits imposed as a friend. Kate, however, reminds Connor at one point that she is an adult and he does not have this authority. Is Connor too controlling? Is Kate rebellious?

*Turn the page for a sneak peek of RITA® Award-winner
Linda Goodnight's heartwarming story,
HOME TO CROSSROADS RANCH.
On sale in March 2009 from Steeple Hill Love Inspired®.*

Chapter One

Nate Del Rio heard screams the minute he stepped out of his Ford F-150 SuperCrew and started up the flower-lined sidewalk leading to Rainy Jernagen's house. He double-checked the address scribbled on the back of a bill for horse feed. Sure enough, this was the place.

Adjusting his Stetson against a gust of March wind, he rang the doorbell, expecting the noise to subside. It didn't.

Somewhere inside the modest, tidy-looking brick house, at least two kids were screaming their heads off in what sounded to his experienced ears like fits of temper. A television blasted out Saturday-morning cartoons—SpongeBob, he thought, though he was no expert on kids' television programs.

He punched the doorbell again. Instead of the expected *ding-dong,* a raucous alternative Christian rock band added a few more decibels to the noise level.

Nate shifted the toolbox to his opposite hand and considered running for his life while he had the chance.

Too late. The bright red door whipped open. Nate's mouth fell open with it.

When the men's ministry coordinator from Bible Fellowship had called him, he'd somehow gotten the impression that he was coming to help a little old schoolteacher. You know, the kind that only drives to school and church and has a big, fat cat.

Not so. The woman standing before him with taffy-blond hair sprouting out from a disheveled ponytail couldn't possibly be any older than his own thirty-one years. A big blotch of something purple stained the front of her white sweatshirt and she was barefooted. Plus, she had a crying baby on each hip and a little red-haired girl hanging on one leg, bawling like a sick calf. And there wasn't a cat in sight.

What had he gotten himself into?

"May I help you?" she asked over the racket. Her blue-gray eyes were little too unfocused and bewildered for his comfort.

Raising his voice, he asked, "Are you Ms. Jernagen?"

"Yes," she said cautiously. "I'm Rainy Jernagen. And you are….?"

"Nate Del Rio."

She blinked, uncomprehending, all the while jiggling both babies up and down. One grabbed a hank of her hair. She flinched, her head angling to one side as she said, still cautiously, "Okaaay."

Nate reached out and untwined the baby's sticky fingers.

A relieved smile rewarded him. "Thanks. Is there something I can help you with?"

He hefted the red toolbox to chest level so she could see it. "From the Handy Man Ministry. Jack Martin called. Said you had a washer problem."

Understanding dawned. "Oh, my goodness. Yes. I'm so sorry. You aren't what I expected. Please forgive me."

She wasn't what he expected, either. Not in the least. Young and with a houseful of kids. He suppressed a shiver. No wonder she looked like the north end of a southbound cow. Kids, even grown ones, could drive a person to distraction. He should know. His adult sister and brother were, at this moment, making his life as miserable as possible. The worst part was they did it all the time. Only this morning his sister, Janine, had finally packed up and gone back to Sal, giving Nate a few days' reprieve.

"Come in, come in," the woman was saying. "It's been a

crazy morning what with the babies showing up at 3:00 a.m. and Katie having a sick stomach. Then while I was doing the laundry, the washing machine went crazy. Water everywhere." She jerked her chin toward the inside of the house. "You're truly a godsend."

He wasn't so sure about that, but he'd signed up for his church's ministry to help single women and the elderly with those pesky little handyman chores like oil changes and leaky faucets. Most of his visits had been to older ladies who plied him with sweet tea and jars of homemade jam and talked about the good old days while he replaced a fuse or unstopped the sink. And their houses had been quiet. Real quiet.

Rainy Jernagen stepped back, motioned him in, and Nate very cautiously entered a room that should have had flashing red lights and a *danger zone* sign.

Toys littered the living room like Christmas morning. An over-turned cereal bowl flowed milk onto a coffee table. Next to a playpen crowding one wall, a green package belched out dispos-able diapers. Similarly, baby clothes were strewn, along with a couple of kids, on the couch and floor. In a word, the place was a wreck.

"The washer is back this way behind the kitchen. Watch your step. It's slippery."

More than slippery. Nate kicked his way through the living room and the kitchen area beyond, though the kitchen actually appeared much tidier than the rest, other than the slow seepage of water coming from somewhere beyond. The shine of liquid glistening on beige tile led them straight to the utility room.

"I turned the faucets off behind the washer when this first started, but a tubful still managed to pump out onto the floor." She hoisted the babies higher on her hip and spoke to a young boy sitting on the floor. "Joshua, get out of those suds."

"But they're pretty, Miss Rainy." The brown-haired boy with bright blue eyes grinned up at her, extending a handful of bubbles. Light reflected off each droplet. "See the rainbows? There's always a rainbow, like you said. A rainbow behind the rain."

Miss Rainy smiled at the child. "Yes, there is. But right now, Mr. Del Rio needs in here to fix the washer. It's a little crowded for all of us." She was right about that. The space was no bigger than a small bathroom. "Can I get you to take the babies to the playpen while I show him around?"

"I'll take them, Miss Rainy." An older boy with a serious face and brown plastic glasses entered the room. Treading carefully, he came forward and took both babies, holding them against his slight chest. Another child appeared behind him. This one a girl with very blond hair and eyes the exact blue of the boy's, the one she'd called Joshua. How many children did this woman have, anyway? Six?

A heavy, smothery feeling pressed against his airway. Six kids?

Before he could dwell on that disturbing thought, a scream of sonic proportions rent the soap-fragrant air. He whipped around ready to protect and defend.

The little blond girl and the redhead were going at it.

"It's mine." Blondie tugged hard on a Barbie doll.

"It's mine. Will said so." To add emphasis to her demand, the redhead screamed bloody murder. "Miss Rainy."

About that time, Joshua decided to skate across the suds, and then slammed into the far wall next to a door that probably opened into the garage. He grabbed his big toe and set up a howl. Water sloshed as Rainy rushed forward and gathered him into her arms.

"Rainy!" Blondie screamed again.

"Rainy!" the redhead yelled.

Nate cast a glance at the garage exit and considered a fast escape. *Lord, I'm here to do a good thing. Can You help me out a little?*

Rainy, her clothes now wet, somehow managed to take the doll from the fighting girls while snuggling Joshua against her side. The serious-looking boy stood in the doorway, a baby on each hip, taking in the chaos.

"Come on, Emma," the boy said to Blondie. "I'll make you some chocolate milk." So they went, slip-sliding out of the flooded room.

Four down, two to go.

Nate clunked his toolbox onto the washer and tried to ignore the chaos. Not an easy task, but one he'd learned to deal with as a boy. As an adult, he did everything possible to avoid this kind of madness. The Lord had a sense of humor sending him to this particular house.

"I apologize, Mr. Del Rio," Rainy said, shoving at the wads of hair that hung around her face like Spanish moss.

"Call me Nate. I'm not that much older than you." At thirty-one and the long-time patriarch of his family, he might feel seventy, but he wasn't.

"Okay, Nate. And I'm Rainy. Really, it's not usually this bad. I can't thank you enough for coming over. I tried to get a plumber, but being Saturday…" She shrugged, letting the obvious go unsaid. No one could get a plumber on the weekend.

"No problem." He removed his white Stetson and placed it next to the toolbox. What was he supposed to say? That he loved wading in dirty soap suds and listening to kids scream and cry? Not likely.

Rainy stood with an arm around each of the remaining children—the rainbow boy and the redhead. Her look of embarrassment had him feeling sorry for her. All these kids and no man around to help. With this many, she'd never find another husband, he was sure of that. Who would willingly take on a boatload of kids?

After a minute, Rainy and the remaining pair left the room and he got to work. Wiggling the machine away from the wall wasn't easy. Even with all the water on the floor, a significant amount remained in the tub. This leftover liquid sloshed and gushed at regular intervals. In minutes, his boots were dark with moisture. No problem there. As a rancher, his boots were often dark with lots of things, the best of which was water.

On his haunches, he surveyed the back of the machine, where

hoses and cords and metal parts twined together like a nest of water moccasins.

As he investigated each hose in turn, he once more felt a presence in the room. Pivoting on his heels, he discovered the two boys squatted beside him, attention glued to the back of the washer.

"A busted hose?" the oldest one asked, pushing up his glasses.

"Most likely."

"I coulda fixed it but Rainy wouldn't let me."

"That so?"

"Yeah. Maybe. If someone would show me."

Nate suppressed a smile. "What's your name?"

"Will. This here's my brother, Joshua." He yanked a thumb at the younger one. "He's nine. I'm eleven. You go to Miss Rainy's church?"

"I do, but it's a big church. I don't think we've met before."

"She's nice. Most of the time. She never hits us or anything, and we've been here for six months."

It occurred to Nate then that these were not Rainy's children. The kids called her Miss Rainy, not Mom, and according to Will they had not been here forever. But what was a young, single woman doing with all these kids?

* * * * *

Look for HOME TO CROSSROADS RANCH
by Linda Goodnight,
on sale March 2009 only from Steeple Hill Love Inspired®,
available wherever books are sold.

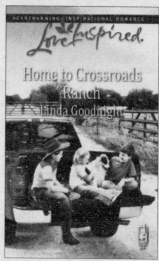

Love Inspired

What do you do when Mr. Right doesn't want kids? Rainy Jernagen and her houseful of foster children won't let a little thing like that get in the way of bringing handyman Nate Del Rio home to them once and for all.

Look for

Home to Crossroads Ranch

by

Linda Goodnight

Available March wherever books are sold, including most bookstores, supermarkets, drugstores and discount stores.

Steeple Hill®

LI87521

REQUEST YOUR FREE BOOKS!

2 FREE RIVETING INSPIRATIONAL NOVELS
PLUS 2 FREE MYSTERY GIFTS

Love Inspired®
SUSPENSE

YES! Please send me 2 FREE Love Inspired® Suspense novels and my 2 FREE mystery gifts (gifts are worth about $10). After receiving them, if I don't wish to receive any more books, I can return the shipping statement marked "cancel". If I don't cancel, I will receive 4 brand-new novels every month and be billed just $4.24 per book in the U.S. or $4.74 per book in Canada, plus 25¢ shipping and handling per book and applicable taxes, if any*. That's a savings of over 20% off the cover price! I understand that accepting the 2 free books and gifts places me under no obligation to buy anything. I can always return a shipment and cancel at any time. Even if I never buy another book, the two free books and gifts are mine to keep forever.   123 IDN ERXX 323 IDN ERXM

Name	(PLEASE PRINT)	
Address		Apt. #
City	State/Prov.	Zip/Postal Code

Signature (if under 18, a parent or guardian must sign)

Order online at www.LoveInspiredSuspense.com
Or mail to Steeple Hill Reader Service:
IN U.S.A.: P.O. Box 1867, Buffalo, NY 14240-1867
IN CANADA: P.O. Box 609, Fort Erie, Ontario L2A 5X3

Not valid to current subscribers of Love Inspired Suspense books.

Want to try two free books from another series?
Call 1-800-873-8635 or visit www.morefreebooks.com

* Terms and prices subject to change without notice. N.Y. residents add applicable sales tax. Canadian residents will be charged applicable provincial taxes and GST. Offer not valid in Quebec. This offer is limited to one order per household. All orders subject to approval. Credit or debit balances in a customer's account(s) may be offset by any other outstanding balance owed by or to the customer. Please allow 4 to 6 weeks for delivery. Offer available while quantities last.

Your Privacy: Steeple Hill Books is committed to protecting your privacy. Our Privacy Policy is available online at www.SteepleHill.com or upon request from the Reader Service. From time to time we make our lists of customers available to reputable third parties who may have a product or service of interest to you. If you would prefer we not share your name and address, please check here. ☐

LISUS08R

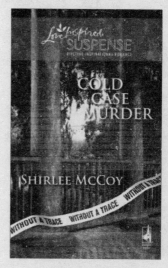

Love Inspired
SUSPENSE

TITLES AVAILABLE NEXT MONTH

Available March 10, 2009

POISONED SECRETS by Margaret Daley
An anonymous tip brought Maggie Ridgeway to her birth
mother. Yet finding her led to more questions. Why did
her parents abandon her? What's triggering the *multiple*
burglaries in her new apartment? Can building owner
Kane McDowell protect her? And once he finds out
who she really is, will he still want to?

COLD CASE MURDER by Shirlee McCoy
Without a Trace

Loomis, Louisiana, holds no charms for Jodie Gilmore. Still,
the novice FBI agent has a job to do, investigating the local
missing person's case. But the job gets complicated when
handsome forensic anthropologist Harrison Cahill uncovers
a decades-old double homicide.

A SILENT TERROR by Lynette Eason
There was no motive for the murder—Marianna Santino's
roommate shouldn't have died. Then Detective
Ethan O'Hara realizes the deaf teacher was the *real*
target. Ethan learns all he can about Marianna. Soon, he's
willing to risk everything—even his heart—to keep her safe.

PERFECT TARGET by Stephanie Newton
The corpse in her path was the first warning. Next was a
break-in at Bayley Foster's home. She's certain that the
stalker who once tormented her has returned to toy with
her again. Her protective neighbor, police detective
Cruse Conyers, is determined to get answers—at any cost.

LISCNMBPA0209